DON'T READ THIS OR YOU MIGHT DIE

Wendy Dalrymple

Copyright © 2023 Wendy Dalrymple

All rights reserved

The characters and events portrayed in this book are fictitious. Any similarity to real persons, living or dead, is coincidental and not intended by the author.

No part of this book may be reproduced, or stored in a retrieval system, or transmitted in any form or by any means, electronic, mechanical, photocopying, recording, or otherwise, without express written permission of the publisher.

Cover design by: WD
Library of Congress Control Number: 2018675309
Printed in the United States of America

CONTENTS

Title Page
Copyright
Chapter One   1
Chapter Two   10
Chapter Three   20
Chapter Four   29
Chapter Five   40
Chapter Six   50
Chapter Seven   61
Chapter Eight   69
Chapter Nine   79
Chapter Ten   89
Chapter Eleven   96
Chapter Twelve   105
Chapter Thirteen   114
Chapter Fourteen   121
Chapter Fifteen   128

Epilogue	134
Books By This Author	137

CHAPTER ONE

Hannah Howarth stood before the gleaming entrance to Tampa Towers on a steamy summer morning, tilting her chin up toward the sky as a droplet of sweat traced down the back of her leg. She clenched her stomach, pressing her portfolio to her chest and shielding her eyes from the harsh sunlight. The Art Deco style building must have been nearly twenty stories high, its entryway boasting a glass pyramid lobby much like the one outside the Louvre. Hannah's destination that morning was located somewhere on the seventeenth floor—the offices of *Visage Magazine*.

A blast of polar air kissed Hannah's damp forehead and neck as the doors to the building parted. Every inch of the entryway was tastefully decorated in chic, clean lines paired with Florida-style flourishes. Furnishings of white marble and metallic gold with lush, leafy accents worked together to create an aesthetic that was one part corporate heaven, one part tropical paradise. The air felt deliciously cool and smelled divine, and brilliant rays of sunshine spilled through the triangular glass panes.

Hannah tucked a long, dark strand of hair

behind her ear as she approached the ash wood and Carrara marble information desk. She forced a smile at the security guard and did her best to radiate an air of confidence. "Excuse me. Can you tell me where the elevators are?"

The indifferent guard kept his gaze glued to his phone as he jerked a thumb over his shoulder. "Over there."

"Thanks." She gave him a sidelong glare, pulled her shoulders back, and walked in the direction he had pointed. Hannah forced herself to refocus as she strode through the lobby toward her destiny, determined to be the personification of poise, capability, and confidence.

Even though the staff writer internship was almost assuredly hers, Hannah was still a bundle of nerves. Her favorite professor in her journalism program at UF was old friends with Grace Hightower, the magazine's notorious editor in chief. Hannah already had someone putting in a good word for the coveted internship, now it was up to her to give a stellar performance. As much as she wanted to write for the elite magazine, the idea of actually working there was beyond intimidating. Grace's razor sharp tongue and icy stare were the stuff of gossip column legend, after all.

Just as her hand reached for the "up" button, the elevator's double doors opened. Hannah blinked at a trio of ultra-stylish, well-dressed thirtysomethings who stared back at her from inside the enclosed space. The first wore a black jumpsuit with a plunging neckline, a cascading waterfall of inky, pin-straight hair falling to a well-defined waist. The second had the cool and artistic air of David Bowie: blonde, androgynous, and lanky in an expertly tailored three-piece suit. The third was a doll-like, effervescent brunette with dark doe eyes in a lavender princess dress. Their collective gaze trailed up and down Hannah's figure in a synchronized wave before they silently pushed past her into the hall.

"Great," she exhaled, stepping into the elevator and pushing the button for the seventeenth floor. The lingering bouquet of their various perfumes and colognes overwhelmed her senses as the elevator door closed, trapping her with notes of wood, vanilla, citrus, florals, and something she couldn't quite place. Hannah scraped her teeth along the length of her tongue to rid herself of the taste.

The doors opened on the seventeenth floor and her pulse kicked up. As she stepped out of the elevator, Hannah was greeted with the unmistakable *Visage* logo emblazoned over yet another reception area. Like the lobby of the building, this space was designed to look futuristic and tropical all at once.

"Welcome to *Visage*. Do you have an appointment?" A striking, model-gorgeous man with a fresh fade and punchy hibiscus print button-down glanced up at her from behind his post. He propped his elbows on the desktop, laced his manicured fingers under his chin, and flashed a smile, revealing a set of flawless teeth.

"Yes," Hannah said, clearing her throat. "I'm supposed to meet Grace Hightower at noon?"

"Ah. Fresh meat." The man raised a duo of artfully microbladed brows. "Name?"

"Hannah. Howarth." She swallowed. Her mouth had suddenly gone bone dry.

He glanced at his computer screen and tapped at his keyboard. He rose from his seat. "This way."

Hannah followed the receptionist down a brightly lit corridor of glass-front offices. The liminal space was a quiet vacuum with only the swish of her polyester pants and twin footsteps to fill the void. They passed what appeared to be a conference room, a set of bathrooms, and a coffee bar and break room before arriving at a set of twelve-foot-high, carved, wooden double doors at the end of the hall.

The receptionist stopped in front of the massive doors and pushed one open. "Take a seat. Ms. Hightower will see you in a minute."

"Thanks."

The door closed behind Hannah as she surveyed the dimly lit interior. The floors were tiled in black travertine and and the windows were draped in dramatic aubergine velvet, blocking out the daylight. Unlike the rest of the building, this room was much more traditional in style with dark wood and black leather furnishings. A sprawling desk sat toward the back of the room under a harsh, abstract painting in gray, black, and white composed in erratic, impasto slashes. The space was somehow cold, sterile, and suffocating all at once.

"You must be Hannah." A woman appeared from behind a darkened doorway, a pair of delicate, pale hands clasped in front of her. Hannah already knew what her would-be editor in chief looked like—everyone in the editorial world did. However, seeing her lush cascade of steel-gray locks, shark-like eyes, and thin, unsmiling lips in the flesh was a surreal and breathtaking experience.

"Ms. Hightower. Thank you for seeing me." Hannah extended her hand.

"Call me Grace." She pursed her lips and glanced at the offered hand, but did not accept it. "Please have a seat."

"Oh. Sure." Heat crept up Hannah's neck as she lowered herself into an overstuffed armchair. She had only been in her prospective new boss's presence for under a minute and was already making social blunders.

"Please excuse the low light. I suffer from migraines." Grace slipped behind her desk and lowered herself into a tufted rolling chair. "So… You were a student of Ingrid's?"

"Yes." Hannah straightened her back and raised her chin. "Professor Applegate was the head of our student newspaper."

"And you were the senior entertainment writer," Grace breathed out a deep sigh. "I enjoyed your article on the re-emergence of nineties trends. Not exactly groundbreaking or transgressive, but cute."

"Thank you."

"Our internship program for the summer is designed to scout fresh new voices in fashion journalism. I'm going to be perfectly honest. I don't think you are the best fit."

"Oh." Hannah glanced down at her plain gray business slacks and white button-down blouse. She didn't typically dress quite so conservatively, but she also didn't think her upcycled, second-hand finds would have been appropriate for an interview either. Maybe she had been wrong.

"Fortunately for you, our last intern unexpectedly quit, and we need quite a bit of help around here. I trust Ingrid's judgment, so if she thinks highly of you, then I'm willing to give this a try."

"You don't have much of a social media presence," Grace continued. "If you hope to stay with *Visage* long-term, I suggest you change that."

"Understood." Hannah's fingers curled around the arms of the chair. Her pulse thrummed in her neck as stars and strobing lights flashed before her eyes. She inhaled sharply and her head swam. All she could manage to do was nod and smile.

"The position pays a small stipend, which also includes boarding if you should require it. We'll need you to start on Monday." Grace cocked her head to one side. "Can you manage that?"

Hannah blinked and snapped back down to Earth. "Yes."

"Good." Grace's lips formed something of a smile. "Do you have a place to stay in town?"

"Not yet."

"See Anton again at the front desk before you leave. Let him know you need a badge and a room at The Palms. We'll have HR begin your paperwork."

"Thank you so much." Hannah stood precariously on newborn giraffe legs. Her instinct was to reach across and shake her new boss's hand, but Grace's attention was already on her laptop.

Hannah showed herself out of the office and was once again bathed in light. The meeting had lasted no more than five minutes, but the intensity of those five minutes had made her feel as though she had aged a decade. Another minute in there and her heart may have exploded. This was it. The job she had been coveting for as long as she could remember. Hannah should have been elated. Instead, she was terrified.

Anton was busy on a call when she returned to the reception desk. He motioned for her to wait a moment as he placed his hand over the phone receiver and whispered to Hannah.

"Be here at nine on Monday." His gaze traveled up and down, and he let out a sigh. "And try to wear something cute? The other writers will crucify you if you show up dressed like that."

He pushed a name badge, key card, and a pamphlet for The Palms extended stay across the desk.

"*Okay*." Her entire body burned as she took her

things. "Thanks."

Hannah sped toward the elevator, adrenaline pumping through her veins. She should have been excited or nervous at the very least. Instead as she pushed the "down" button, all Hannah felt was dread. Writing for *Visage* had been her dream ever since she stole her first copy of the magazine from a grocery store when she was eleven. But she was miles away from home and down to her last two hundred bucks. Even though she wasn't completely confident about the internship, she didn't have many other options than to take it. Going home to Omega, Georgia with her tail between her legs wasn't an option either.

She glanced down at her keycard and the pamphlet to The Palms as the elevator doors opened again. The same trio of well-dressed individuals passed her again, this time brandishing hot beverages and pastry boxes. Hannah kept her head down and walked quickly as they passed her. Her stomach made a grumble of complaint, and she sent up a silent prayer that The Palms had a well-stocked continental breakfast and a swimming pool. Even if the position at *Visage* was unbearable, she would have a soft place to land for a while.

Though the hotel was only a mile away, Hannah contemplated calling a cab as she stood on the sidewalk under the scorching midday sun. She decided to save what was left of her meager funds and suffer the walk. She glanced up at the building toward what she thought would be the seventeenth floor for one last look at the place where she would be working that summer. From one of the windows, she could swear she saw four silhouettes staring down at her. Watching. Waiting.

CHAPTER TWO

Hannah's weekend of comfort and bliss at The Palms hotel was regretfully short-lived. The days sped by in a blur of air conditioning, unlimited television, and clean sheets. She enjoyed the buffet of breakfast treats and lazy afternoons by the pool, reveling in all the little luxuries she was rarely afforded. On Saturday, she walked to a thrift store downtown in search of a few affordable pieces of clothes to wear to work. She managed to find three dresses, two pairs of pants, four blouses, a blazer, and a pair of black heels all for under a hundred dollars. On Sunday, she hand-washed her new work wardrobe in the hotel room bathtub while reruns of *Friends* played in the background.

    Hannah walked the mile from The Palms to Tampa Towers on the first official day of her internship, pushing down a mountain of anxiety. It would likely be two weeks until she received a paycheck, and while she was thankful that she had a place to stay, living in the city and keeping up appearances was going to be expensive. She forced a smile and hoped that her thrifted wardrobe and drugstore makeup would pass amongst her peers. Hannah was used to blending in with the background and hiding in plain sight, but something told her that she wasn't going to get away with lurking in the shadows at *Visage*.

"*Much* better." Anton stood and smiled as Hannah approached the reception desk. He motioned toward her ensemble. "Is that Elie Tahari?"

She glanced down at her ruffled floral dress. "No. It's vintage."

"Oh," Anton made a soft huffing sound and turned on his heels. "Follow me. I'll show you to your desk."

Hannah followed behind him once again, only this time the office space was slightly more alive. As they passed the glass-front offices, it became apparent to her that everyone who worked at the fashion magazine looked like they could have been models themselves. With every step she took, Hannah's gut sank further and further. She was a fraud. She had no business being there. She...

"This is your cubicle. You'll have to share with Hector; he's our photography intern." Anton yawned and pointed toward a small, dark corner. "I'll let Valerie know you're here, and she can get you up to speed."

"Thanks." Hannah shrugged off her purse as Anton disappeared down the hall. The cubicle was nothing like the other glass-front offices with sweeping views of Tampa Bay; this space was dark and cramped with no window and only enough room for two desks and two chairs. It was the perfect place to hide shabbily-dressed, inexperienced interns. Hannah sat at the empty desk and surveyed her new work space as an unfamiliar voice boomed through the air.

"And if Steven thinks I'm going to drive all the way to Sarasota to take a picture of some bird, then he's got another thing coming." A man near Hannah's age entered the cubicle with a cell phone pressed to his ear. He pushed a pair of clear plastic frames up his nose and leaned against the cubicle entryway. "Hey, I'll call you back."

"Hi." She smiled and held up her hand in a timid wave.

"You must be Hannah." He tucked his phone into the back pocket of his jeans and extended a hand. "Hector Gonzalez. Guess we're gonna be cube mates."

"Nice to meet you." She grinned and shook his hand. A wave of relief washed over her as he returned with a friendly smile and gave her hand a warm, firm shake.

"Sorry about that. I won't take my personal calls in here now that we're sharing a space."

"It doesn't bother me," Hannah said. "What was that about a bird, though?"

"I was telling my girlfriend that I might have to take a road trip for a photo shoot next week." He shrugged. "Stephen wants me to drive an hour away to take a picture of some rare bird for a footwear photo shoot. Seems like a waste of gas and time to me."

"Oh no," Hannah grimaced.

"I don't mean to be negative." Hector flopped into his seat across from hers. "It's just... working for *Visage* can be *intense*. I hope you're ready for it."

"Ready as I'll ever be."

"Knock knock." A singsong voice filled the air, and Hannah jumped in her seat. The effervescent brunette from the elevator stood at the entryway of their cubicle looking like a high fashion frosted cupcake. Her hair was piled high into a beehive, and she wore a pastel rainbow dress with a full skirt and a sweetheart neckline. "Are you Hannah?"

Hanna blinked and nodded. "Hi."

"Valerie Beauregard," she said, her voice dripping with honey. She held out a manicured pink hand and smiled. "But don't call me Val. I hate that."

Hannah held out her hand as well and felt something smooth and rectangular beneath her grip. She frowned as their hands parted and a twenty dollar bill was left in her palm. She glanced back up at Valerie under furrowed brows.

"We're gonna need you to go get our coffee for the morning meeting. If you scoot across the street to Caffeine, they know our order by heart. Just tell them it's for *Visage*." Valerie looked over at Hector and pursed her lips, then returned her gaze to Hannah. "Bring them to Grace's office when you get back, okay?"

She stared at the cash in her hand and then back at Valerie. "Uh, sure I guess."

"Thanks, babe! See you in a few." Valerie turned, leaving a sickly trail of cotton candy scented perfume in her wake.

Hannah snorted and glanced over at Hector. "Seriously?"

"I told you." He shrugged and placed a set of noise-canceling headphones over his ears. "*Intense.*"

"I'll be back, I guess." She sighed and grabbed her bag. Hannah knew she would be expected to do the crappy grunt work that the senior writers didn't want to do, but this? Fetching coffee for her superiors was just far too cliché.

Her cheeks burned as she passed a smirking Anton and stepped into the elevator. She tried to remind herself that this was what she wanted. She needed a place to stay, a job, the editorial credits... all of it. Hannah just needed to survive the summer, but there was only so much abuse she was willing to take. She glanced at the cash in the palm of her hand and knew deep down that this little chore would only be the beginning.

❋ ❋ ❋

Hannah knocked on the wooden double doors to Grace's office later that morning, her arms overflowing with coffee and pastries. Her heart raced as she juggled their food and drink; the back of her neck was damp with sweat from hoofing it across the street. She clenched her teeth and reminded herself to breathe as she waited to be let in.

"Come in." The editor's steely voice pierced through the double doors.

Hannah struggled to balance the beverage carrier and pastry bags as she pulled on the handle to the heavy wooden door. The order at Caffeine had well exceeded the twenty dollars that Valerie had given her and included one vanilla latte, one hazelnut latte, one macchiato, one black coffee, two lemon scones, and one cinnamon roll. Panic left a metallic taste in her mouth as she paid for the remaining balance of the coffee run with what little money was left in her account. She squinted as she entered the room, allowing her eyes to adjust to the low light. It didn't take long for her to recognize the trio sitting in a semi-circle across from Grace's desk.

"Please. Join us." Grace stood at her desk and beckoned for her to come closer. Her crisp white button-down glowed in the darkened room, and her long, steely locks fell loose around her shoulders.

"Where should I put these?" Hannah nodded toward the coffee and baked goods.

"I'll take that." The woman with long, dark hair rose from her seat, bringing with her the scent of cinnamon and clove. Her voice was deep and husky, and she was dressed in a long-sleeve leopard print jumpsuit and spike heels. Up close, her skin glowed golden and perfect; her eyes two dark intimidating pools rimmed with an impeccable wing of black liner.

"Thanks, Selena," Valerie twittered and

accepted the vanilla latte and cinnamon roll.

Selena, of the leopard print suit, took the macchiato and a lemon scone. She examined the macchiato and extended it to the androgynous blonde. "Fox, I think this is for you. Did you get a scone?"

"Yeah. Thanks." Fox took the coffee and scone, their slim wrists poking out from under an oversized blazer. Even in the near dark, Hannah noted that Fox sported dozens of tattoos.

Selena handed Grace the plain black coffee and returned to her seat.

Valerie pouted at Hannah. "Did you get something for yourself?"

"I don't drink coffee," Hannah replied.

"Oh," Selena said, "that's weird."

"Take a seat, Hannah. We were just going over the layout for October." Grace placed a pair of reading glasses on the bridge of her nose.

"The um... the coffee and pastries cost more than what you gave me?" Hannah lowered herself into her seat and glanced at Valerie.

The room fell silent as all eyes turned toward her. Fox smirked and let out a low chuckle. Adrenaline pushed through Hannah's veins as she stared back at her new co-workers. She was a defenseless little bunny in a pit of vipers.

Grace shot the senior writers an ice-cold look. "That's enough."

"Oh, sorry!" Valerie said, her voice more of a whine than an apology. "Just ask Anton to pay you back from petty cash."

"Okay." Hannah folded her hands in her lap.

"If we have the very important business of coffee out of the way, I would like to start talking about denim trends for fall." Grace leaned her palms on her desk and glared out at the room of writers.

"Yes, Grace," they all chimed.

The hair on Hannah's arms stood on end. There was something off about the meeting, about her co-workers... about *everything*. She sat in the dark and remained quiet, taking notes and wishing she could disappear as she listened to her new team. It didn't take long for Hannah to figure out that Valerie was the senior fashion writer, in charge of ready-to-wear and runway trends. Selena, the senior beauty writer, was in charge of reporting on the latest hair and makeup news. Fox, the senior writer for footwear and accessories, sought out jewelry, handbags, and shoes to showcase on the glossy pages of *Visage*. Then there was Grace, the maestro of it all, calling the shots and bringing everything together in her vision. Hannah wasn't quite sure where she would fit into the equation, but hoped that there would be more to her role at *Visage* than fetching coffee and acting as a human doormat.

"So, what do you think Hannah? Are wide-leg jeans going to be making a comeback?" Grace lowered her reading glasses and glanced at her from across the room. Hannah's pulse pounded in her neck. Jeans? What did Hannah really know about jeans anyway?

"Um, trend forecasts show that low-rise jeans sales are picking up, actually." Hannah cleared her throat. "Wide-leg jeans are becoming slightly less popular as street style begins to favor low-rise jeans."

"Ew." Valerie sipped her coffee. "No one is going to want to wear low-rise jeans again."

"I mean, she has a point." Fox said. "No one thought mom jeans would be back, but people love 'em."

"Valerie. Put some low-rise jeans on the denim trends spread." Grace returned her reading glasses to the bridge of her nose.

Valerie glared at Hannah from across the room. "Fine."

The knot in Hannah's stomach tightened. She could feel the animosity seething from her new co-workers, and she didn't blame them. Why in the world would Grace trust Hannah's judgment with something so important as denim forecast trends on her first day?

"Okay, so that just leaves new makeup trends. Selena, come up with something fabulous for me by the end of the day?"

"Sure." Selena nodded.

"All right. We'll circle back again for the afternoon meeting." Grace glanced at Fox. "Would you help Hannah get her computer set up? Have her rehash some article on canvas sneakers or something."

"Got it, boss." Fox smirked and gave Grace a

salute.

"Okay, team." Grace said. "Time to get to work."

CHAPTER THREE

"Here, just look through the September and October issues from the last three years. You should get a pretty good idea of what Grace is looking for." Fox picked out six thick magazines from the *Visage* library and handed them over to Hannah. "Just write, like, a thousand words on why it's cute to wear sneakers with overalls and dresses and blah, blah, blah. Oh, and make sure to bring four copies of your article to Grace's office for our afternoon meeting."

"Sneakers? Isn't that topic a little… *pedestrian* for *Visage*?" Hannah glanced at Fox with a skeptical frown as she struggled to keep the glossy, thick magazines from slipping through her arms.

Fox shrugged. "Nah. Grace is kind of going for a younger vibe these days. High fashion is gauche. Streetwear and Gen Z fashion is in."

"Oh. Okay, thanks." She gulped and glanced back toward her cubicle. "So, is there, like, a training manual or anything I need to read?"

Fox ruffled their mane of shaggy bleached layers, squinted, and then locked eyes with Hannah. "Did Grace say something to you about a training manual?"

"No. I just wondered. Since it's my first day and all…."

"Right." Fox sucked in a breath. "Well, I'm right over there if you have any questions. The IT department should have left a set of instructions for you to sign on to your system."

"Wait, but should I…."

"Good luck. You'll need it." With that, the footwear and accessories senior writer disappeared into an adjacent glass-front cubicle and closed the door behind them.

"Thanks," Hannah scoffed.

Her chest felt as if the wind had been knocked out of her. She turned toward the dark, cramped, desk drowning in defeat. She had guessed that her internship position would mean being thrown to the wolves, but she hadn't expected to receive zero training. Now with her first assignment looming, the pressure was mounting. She placed the stack of magazines on her desk, slipped into her seat, and let out a long, slow breath.

"Hey. How ya holding up?" Hector turned and flashed her a friendly, empathetic smile.

"You're right. They're brutal," Hannah groaned and glanced over at Hector's desk. Her lips spread into a half grin as she took in his decor: a blend of Star Wars trinkets, Lord of the Rings memorabilia, and a poster for some band she had never heard of.

Hannah spied a photo of Hector and a smiling woman taped under his monitor. "Is that your girlfriend?"

Hector's face lit up. "Yeah. That's Alicia."

"Is she a photographer too?"

"Nah. She's a yoga instructor. She's into a bunch of woo-woo stuff. Thankfully, she likes Star Wars at least," Hector laughed and shrugged. "You got someone too?"

Hannah shook her head. "No. I'm happily single."

"That's cool," Hector said. "You from around here?"

"Not exactly. I went to school at the University of Florida. I'm originally from Georgia, though." Hannah's shoulders relaxed. It was a relief to be able to talk to someone without having her guard up.

"I grew up in Tampa," Hector said. "Over in Ybor."

"Really? I've been meaning to check it out down there."

"My great-grandpa managed one of the cigar factories." Hector pulled a black and white photo from the board behind his monitor and handed it to her. "See, right there? That night club used to be his place."

"Oh wow. You took this?" Hannah examined the photo. "Hey, you're pretty good."

"Good enough to take pictures of models and handbags, I guess," he shrugged. "Anyway, you have an assignment already?"

"Yeah. Writing about shoes," Hannah sighed, glancing back at her computer. "Hector, can I ask you something?"

"Sure."

"What's up with the senior writers?" Hannah leaned in and lowered her voice to a whisper. "They seem kinda... standoffish."

"Oh, you mean the Corporate Coven?"

"The what?"

"The Corporate Coven. That's my nickname for them." He shook his head. "Look, it's not just you. They treat *everyone* like they don't exist."

"Why?"

"Who knows?" Hector snorted. "It's a power trip thing, I guess."

"I suppose I should get started on my assignment." Hannah glanced back at her computer and sighed, not looking forward to her task at hand. *Visage* was the epitome of grace and beauty; all she had wanted to do since she was a little girl was to work for the upscale fashion magazine. Now that she was here, she wasn't so sure.

"Yeah, these image edits are due by lunch." Hector raised his eyebrows. "Welcome to the team."

"Thanks." Hannah smiled, thankful that at least her cubicle mate was friendly.

She powered on her computer and glanced at the time. It was already nearly eleven a.m., and her stomach groaned as she reached for her bag and pulled out a granola bar and an apple that she had snatched from the breakfast buffet at the hotel. She had four hours to write the perfect article on canvas sneakers—an article meant to impress her fellow writers and please her boss. Maybe even earn her a little respect. Hannah laced her fingers together and relished the sound of her knuckles cracking as she set to work.

※ ※ ※

The minutes turned into hours on Hannah's desktop computer clock as she pored over back issues and outlined her article on canvas shoes. She worked diligently through lunch, setting up her email, contacting IT, and getting to know her new work station before finally setting to the task of writing. She already knew the format and tone of the magazine like the back of her hand, but it was imperative that she nail this first assignment. *Visage* had been her secret bible all throughout her sheltered teen years, and she needed to show that she had the teeth to keep up with her peers. As the end of the day neared, she finally completed a feature article on canvas sneakers that she felt confident enough to show to Grace and the senior writers.

Grace's office was cool and dark as Hannah entered with four fresh copies of her article titled "Sneak These into Your Wardrobe" in hand. It wasn't her best work, but she was still confident that she had come up with some new ideas for what was essentially the most common fashion item in existence. More than anything, Hannah was terrified of facing the firing squad of senior writers.

"Selena, were you able to secure samples of the dark-pigment lipsticks?" Grace lowered her reading glasses as Hannah took her seat.

"Yes," Selena nodded. "Matte shades are perfect for fall. I added a few shimmers and glosses too for that nineties throwback vibe."

"Excellent." Grace held out her hand. "Hannah, did you bring the footwear feature?"

Hannah nodded and approached Grace's desk. She glanced down at the smooth, black desktop, trying to spot any clues about the *Visage* editor in chief's personality. Just like every other corner of the office, Grace's desk was immaculate and ornate all at once. No family photos. No funny coffee mugs. Not a single tchotchke in sight. A slim laptop was the only evidence of anything modern in the entire room.

"Thank you, Hannah." Grace smiled and accepted her printed article. "Pass one out to your team members as well."

Hannah turned and gave a copy of her footwear article to Valerie, Fox, and Selena. Each of them accepted the page with indifference. Her face went numb as she returned to her seat like a death row prisoner awaiting the executioner.

"Hmm." Grace readjusted her reading glasses and nodded. After a moment, she made another breathy noise through her nose and turned to Valerie. "This is good. Just cut out the third paragraph and print it."

"What?" Fox sputtered. "You can't be seri...."

Grace's eyes flashed as she stared down

the footwear and accessories senior writer. For a moment, Hannah could have sworn she heard something of a snarl echo through the room.

Selena crossed her legs and chuckled.

Valerie coughed and sat up straight. "Fox already submitted enough footwear articles for the October issue."

"Cut one out then," Grace snipped and turned her steely gaze to Valerie. "Will there be anything else?"

"No, ma'am." Valerie's shoulders curled inward. Her entire being seemed to wilt like a flower after sunset.

"Good." Grace smiled. "Selena, tomorrow I need you to oversee Hannah and Hector at the Curvature photo shoot."

Selena's smirking expression fell. "Yes, ma'am."

"That's all I have for today, then. See you tomorrow." Grace swiveled in her chair and returned her focus to her laptop without regarding Hannah or the senior writers again.

Selena, Fox, and Valerie all rose from their seats and walked out the door single file. Hannah followed them automatically, her body thrumming with a cocktail of panic-inducing, fight-or-flight chemicals. She could barely contain the excitement that threatened to bubble to the surface as she pushed through the heavy, wooden double doors and out into the light. She was going to get a byline. In *Visage Magazine.* It was a dream come true.

Valerie turned to face Hannah once they passed the threshold of Grace's office and displayed a saccharine smile. "Congratulations, Hannah. Interns rarely get printed."

"Thank you. I really wasn't expecting…."

"Don't get used to it," Selena cut in and pointed a stiletto nail in her face.

"A fucking *feature*!" Fox spat, their voice acid.

Hannah jerked back as anger and a primordial fear coursed through every cell of her being. She was surrounded, an injured baby gazelle lost in the savannah with hyenas closing in. Only, Hannah was tired of being a wounded animal. She stared at their perfect, enraged features and remembered how hard she had worked to get where she was. *No*. She wasn't going to be intimidated. Not this time. Hannah squared her shoulders, straightened her back, and smacked Selena's hand away.

"Don't ever put your finger in my face again," Hannah said slowly and deliberately. Her pulse was slower now as she faced Fox. "Sorry if Grace likes my writing. Don't take it too personally."

Hannah pushed her way through the well-dressed barricade of writers toward her cubicle, a triumphant grin set on her lips. She didn't give them a second glance, but she could still feel their eyes boring into the back of her head. She imagined them watching her sashay away, mouths agape and frothing with anger. It was an image she would hold on to.

"How did it go?" Hector lowered his

headphones and turned to her.

Hannah picked up her bag and nodded. "Really well. Grace is going to print my feature."

He held up a hand. "Hey, congrats!"

She slapped him a high five. "I almost can't believe it."

"Well, believe it. Grace doesn't hand out praise to just anyone."

"I figured as much." Hannah took in a deep breath and hazarded a look into the hallway. The Corporate Coven had disbanded to their offices. "I guess I'm going to be on assignment with you and Selena tomorrow."

"That should be fun," he snorted. "Selena is usually okay to work with. She ignores me for the most part."

"I wish I could say the same." She picked up her bag and turned off her computer monitor. "I'm heading out for the day. See you tomorrow."

"See you," Hector said, grabbing his headphones. "Oh, and Hannah?"

"Yeah?"

"Seriously. Watch your back with them."

"I will." Hannah nodded and gave him a reassuring smile. "It might be them that has to look out for *me*."

CHAPTER FOUR

"Dammit, Hector. *No*! Grace hates cutesy shit. You know that."

Selena stomped onto the Curvature photo shoot set the following day and grabbed a pink teddy bear with her pointed fingernails. Her dagger-like manicure punctured the plush, velvety exterior of the stuffed toy before she tossed it over her shoulder. The curvy model decked out in a matching hot pink camisole, garter belt, and fishnet tights gave her a terrified, wide-eyed stare.

"Sorry, Selena." Hector winced and lowered his camera. "Stephen usually lets me add my own props."

"Karina, arch your back and stick out your ass! *Jesus*, do I have to do everything?" Selena readjusted a light shade and stomped off set. "Valerie should be the one dealing with this bullshit. This is the last time I'm babysitting interns, I swear."

Hannah watched, frozen, as Hector kneeled and began to photograph the scantily-clad lingerie model again. They were nearly finished with their all-day photo shoot for the Curvature full-figured lingerie spread, and up until that point, things had gone smoothly. Hannah's task for the day was to take notes and fetch coffee and lunch orders while staying out of the way. She had managed to hover blissfully in the background up to that point, but now as the photo shoot was wrapping up, Selena's true nature shone through, dark and full of venom.

"Hannah, make yourself useful. Get in there."

"What," Hannah asked, exchanging glances with Hector, "you want me in the shoot?"

"*Yes*. What the fuck else do you think I mean?" Selena hissed. "This setup isn't nearly edgy enough. We need a different angle."

Hannah glanced down at her outfit for the day. She liked the polka-dot blouse and navy slacks combo that she had cobbled together from the thrift store, but she was nowhere near camera-ready. Her hair was a mess. Her makeup had melted off by that point. There was no way that any photo Hector would take of her could possibly go to print.

"I'm not camera-ready."

Selena rolled her eyes. "Go put on one of the Curvature pieces then. *Duh*."

Hannah gritted her teeth and walked on adrenaline-numb legs to the changing room. She didn't need her gut instincts to tell her that the current situation was wrong and that she was being taken advantage of. Any other self-respecting person would have left and refused to be treated that way. But Hannah was beyond broke. She had no home to go to. No one to help guide her. Besides, this job meant more to her than just security and stability. She owed it to herself to stick it out—

she owed it to the little girl who would hide away tattered copies of *Visage* under her bed. She owed it to that strange, small voice that always told her that this was all going to be hers some day. She just had to put in the work. She had to take the abuse. She had to *wait*.

Hannah rummaged around in the samples from Curvature and found a black negligee that offered the most coverage possible. Her conservative upbringing reinforced her sense of self-consciousness, but the idea of showing too much flesh didn't completely repel her. She just wanted it to be on her own terms. Hannah stared at herself in the mirror and frowned. She wasn't ready. Maybe she would never be. She smoothed down her hair, applied a layer of lipstick and a swipe of mascara from Selena's sample makeup kit, and steadied herself for what was to come.

When Hannah returned, Karina was sitting on the couch and scrolling through her phone. Selena and Hector were hunched over the camera looking at the shots he had already taken. Hannah stepped onto the set and all eyes turned to her. Selena's lower lip fell open, her eyes wide. Hector gave Hannah a look that she read as pity. Hannah didn't want to do this, but being assertive was never her strong point. She cleared her throat and closed her eyes. Time to try and reason with the unreasonable.

"My hair and makeup aren't editorially ready," Hannah said. "We're running out of time and I don't want to overbook Karina."

"Your hair and makeup are fine," Selena crossed her arms. "Besides, Grace is trying to go for a more grungy street look these days. It'll work."

"But, Selena. I'm not comfortable…."

"Just do it!" Selena's eyes flashed, her voice shrill and piercing.

Hannah held her breath and looked to Hector. She trembled and hated herself at that moment. She was a tiny bunny rabbit. A scared mouse. A helpless little baby.

"It's okay," Hector reassured her. "Let's just get this over with."

Hannah exchanged a look of confusion with Karina. Every bit of the situation they were being put in felt wrong and unprofessional, but once again, Hannah was trapped. She couldn't say no.

Hannah walked toward the velvet chaise lounge and turned to Selena. "What do you want me to do?"

"Get down on all fours," Selena smirked. "Both of you."

Karina kneeled and placed both palms on the floor. Hannah lowered herself to the floor on wobbly legs and mirrored her stance.

"Now face each other," Selena ordered. "Hector, get a tight shot of this."

"Like this?" Karina scooted closer. Her lips were mere inches from Hannah's.

"Yeah. Both of you arch your backs."

Hector lowered his camera. "I don't think this

is...."

"Don't be a little bitch, *Hector*. Just do it," Selena ordered. "This is perfect. Just like what you wrote in your feature. Right, Hannah? *The ideal juxtaposition of highbrow and lowbrow*."

Hannah's face flamed. The zip snap of Hector's camera lens whizzed through the air. Flash-bangs of light captured her humiliation, forever suspended in digital form. She and Karina stayed in that uncomfortably close position, backs arched and eyes locked, for what felt like an eternity.

"Karina," Selena chuckled and barked out another order, "put your fingers in her mouth."

Hannah rose to her knees, panting, "that's enough."

"Yeah, this is bullshit," Karina stood and helped Hannah to her feet. "I'm done."

"Fine. I think we have everything we need anyway." Selena's phone rang. She answered the call with a smirk. "Hey. Yeah, we're just wrapping up here."

Karina snatched her silk robe from behind the chaise lounge and frowned at Hector. "I'm going to complain to my manager about this."

"I think you should. I'm so sorry." Hector wiped his brow with the back of his hand. "I'm going to delete these."

"Good." Karina pulled a phone from her robe pocket and stormed off the set.

"What the hell was that?" Hannah sat on the velvet chaise and placed a hand on her forehead.

"One of their infamous power trips," he said. "I'm sorry. I shouldn't have let that happen."

"It's not your fault." Hannah leaned forward and propped her elbows on the top of her thighs. "I don't know if I'm cut out for this work."

"That makes two of us." Hector glanced over his shoulder. "She's coming back."

Selena glided back onto the set and tucked her phone into her purse. The green silk jumpsuit that she'd worn to the shoot that day featured a plunging neckline that nearly grazed her navel and only made her look more serpent-like. "I'm out. Clean all this up."

"That wasn't cool." Hannah stood and faced her. "I should report you to HR."

Selena's full black lashes lowered in a slow blink. She shrugged, her lips set into a smug grin. "Go for it. I'm not worried."

"You should be."

"Whatever." Selena rolled her eyes, turned, and walked away, leaving Hannah and Hector to clean up.

"Great," Hector scoffed and began to break down light shades.

"Can't you say something to your supervisor?" Hannah asked, folding up an umbrella.

"Nah. He's just as bad as they are," Hector sighed. "I only have to put up with this for a few more weeks and then I'm outta here."

"Did you get a job offer?"

"Not exactly. I've decided to start freelancing

full-time. I already take pictures at beach weddings and stuff on the side. Business is finally picking up though," he said. "You should think about getting out too."

"I don't have anywhere else to go." She handed him a folding light stand. "This was supposed to be my big break."

"Yeah, well, it just might break you instead."

Hannah changed back into her clothes, helped Hector put away the studio equipment and checked the time on her phone. It was well after four p.m.; she had missed the afternoon meeting. The fact was relieving and insulting all at once. From the moment she had stepped foot in the Tampa Towers building, she had suspected that she was already marked as lower-class by the senior writers. An outcast. *Other*. It was something she was used to. Still, Hannah was determined not to let them beat her. She had goals and aspirations that were bigger than *Visage* magazine.

"Do you have any plans for dinner?" Hector asked as they returned to their shared work space. "My girlfriend is a vegetarian, so that means I am too. When I'm at home, anyway. It's taco night and we always make too much."

"I'd love tacos," Hannah smiled. "I've had nothing but free hotel breakfast for the last four days."

"Oh, you're definitely coming over then. What's your number? I'll text you the address." He handed over his phone. She entered her phone number and name into his contact list. "Thanks. I don't really know anyone in town. I appreciate it."

"No prob." Hector scrunched his nose and made a face. "Ew. Do you smell that?"

Hannah sniffed the air outside their cubicle. "Yeah. It smells like…."

She peered into their shared workspace. A small white pastry box sat on Hannah's chair, one that looked suspiciously like it came from the café across the street. Hannah and Hector exchanged confused glances as she picked up the box and read the hanging tag. "*Eat Me.*"

Hannah opened the box. She gagged, closed the lid, and put the box on her desk.

"What is it?" Hector reached over and lifted the lid. "Oh my god. Is that… *human*?"

"I don't know, but I need to get rid of it." Hannah held her nose and picked up the trash can. Her ears twitched. Down the hallway the gentle sound of cackling tinkled in the air.

"That's so fucking gross!" Hector shouted.

"I know. I'll call a janitor I guess." Hannah's face was on fire as she dumped the horrific smelling box into her trash can. She double knotted the top of the trash bag then slathered her hands in antibacterial hand sanitizer. "I'm going to Grace."

"Grace? Why?"

"It's obvious that one of the senior writers left this for me," Hannah said, picking up the trash can. "I may look like a doormat, but I'm not going to let them treat me like one."

"Oh, God. I gotta get out of here." Hector made a gurgling, choking sound and picked up his backpack. "Text me later and come over for dinner if you still have an appetite."

"Will do. Thanks, Hector."

Hannah scooped up her trash can, stinking present and all, and marched toward Grace's office. She didn't care whether or not she got fired. She didn't care about her byline, her reputation, she didn't care about anything. At that moment, all she wanted was retribution. Justice. *Revenge*. She rapped on the exterior of the large double doors with more force than usual.

"Come in." Grace's voice was melodious on the other side of the door.

Hannah pushed her way into the darkened space, seething. Grace was dressed simply again that day in a long-sleeved gray tunic dress. She folded her hands on top of her desk with one perfectly groomed eyebrow arched high as Hannah approached.

"I'm sorry to burst in like this, Grace, but I need to talk to you."

"The team is giving you trouble, aren't they?" Grace nodded, closing her eyes and letting out a long sigh. "I suspected they might. I'm sorry."

"Oh." Hannah placed the trash can on the floor, embarrassed now that she had even thought to bring it in. "Yes. They've been awful to me. They left something disgusting at my desk. I think I should file a report with HR."

"No need for that. I'll set them straight," Grace tutted and shook her head. She bent down, opened a drawer on the right side of her desk, and pulled out a thick book bound in black leather. She caressed the cover, smiled, and extended it toward Hannah. "Here."

"What's this?" Hannah took the book, its cover was warm and soft like a sheepskin glove. She liked the weight of it in her hand.

"It's the official *Visage* handbook. I only give them out to my senior writers and associates." Grace's lips spread into a sort of smile.

"A style book?" she asked, opening the front cover.

"Something like that," Grace said. "You may have noticed that *Visage* is a special place. We do things very differently around here."

Hannah glanced down at the front page. It was printed in a text with characters she didn't recognize. She glanced back at Grace with a quizzical expression.

"If you're going to survive here at *Visage*, you need to give as good as you get," Grace explained. "Hannah, are you up to the challenge?"

The atmosphere around Hannah crackled with electricity. Her gut dropped and the sensation of falling came over her, as though she were standing at the edge of a cliff. She closed the cover and was overwhelmed by the aroma of flowers, the taste of metal in her mouth, a high-pitched ringing in her ear.

"Hannah. Are you still with me?"

Hannah opened her eyes. Everything was clear again. She breathed in low and slow and deep. "Yes."

"Memorize the handbook." Grace nodded. "Follow your instincts. You'll find your place here at *Visage*."

"Thank you." Something fluttered inside her chest as she picked up the trash can, turned, and walked out of Grace's office in a trance. She tucked the handbook under her arm and passed a janitor vacuuming in the hallway. Hannah dumped the entire contents of the trash can into the janitor's wheeled trolly and returned to her cubicle. Hector was already gone for the day, as was everyone else, and only the hum of the vacuum filled the empty office.

Hannah placed the handbook in her purse and glanced at the carpeted floor. There was a single dead cockroach at the entrance to her and Hector's shared cubicle. The roach was turned on its back with its feet in the air and wiry little legs bent at an angle. With Grace's words bouncing around her skull, she plucked the cockroach off the carpet between her index finger and thumb to examine the shiny brown insect. She knew exactly where it should go. Hannah entered Selena's darkened office, the space still smelling of her spicy cinnamon clove perfume. She placed the cockroach on the keyboard and smiled.

CHAPTER FIVE

"Hey, you made it!" Hector opened the door to apartment 3A later that evening, welcoming Hannah with the savory aroma of cumin and other warm spicesa. His apartment in downtown Tampa was thankfully within walking distance of her hotel, though in an older, less developed part of town. Still, as soon as she crossed the threshold, Hannah felt warmed and welcomed.

Hannah kicked off her shoes by the entrance. "Thanks for inviting me. It smells amazing in here."

A tall woman with her hair pinned back in a handkerchief greeted her. Hannah immediately recognized her from Hector's desktop photo. "Hi, I'm Alicia. You must be Hannah."

"Nice to meet you. Thank you so much for inviting me."

"Hector said you two had a pretty rough day."

"Yeah." Hannah rolled her eyes. "I knew that an internship would be intimidating, but the way we were treated today was out of line."

"Hector said someone left a "present" for you at your desk?" Alicia frowned and made a disgusted expression.

"Yeah," Hannah scoffed. "I have an idea of who it was. Don't worry, I left them a little present too."

"Nice." Hector smiled. "You want a beer?"

"No, thank you. I don't really drink," Hannah said. "I'm excited for tacos though."

"Good. Let's go eat." Alicia wound her arm through Hannah's and guided her to their little eat-in kitchen.

Hannah scanned the space and smiled appreciatively at Hector and Alicia's blended life; they were an odd couple, to be sure, with her tie-dye wall-hangings and macrame and his black-and-white photography and Star Wars decor. Still, the modest apartment had the comfortable appearance of two struggling post-grad students in love. Hector assembled three plates as Hannah and Alicia chatted and got to know each other. Soon they were all laughing and stuffing their faces with seitan-filled corn tortillas.

"Thank you again for inviting me," Hannah said, helping herself to a fourth tortilla. "I'm kind of on a budget. I haven't had a hot meal in a while."

"We know how it is," Alicia said. "Hector and I both work gig jobs and commissions, so cash isn't always consistent. But we get to do what we love, so that's more important."

"Yeah." Hannah agreed. "I thought writing for a magazine was what I wanted to do, but now I'm not so sure."

"Well I suspect that things would be different at another magazine." Hector nodded. "*Visage* is just… something else."

Hannah swallowed her last bite of taco, took a sip of water, then bit her lower lip. The handbook had been burning a hole in her handbag from the moment she left the office. The way it molded to her hand, the surge of power that coursed through her as she held it… it had frightened and intrigued her all at once. She didn't have anyone else to talk to about it. Hector was the only one who she could confide in.

She took a deep breath and stared at their kitchen table. "Grace gave me a handbook today."

Hector sputtered and wiped a trickle of foamy beer from his nose. "What? Like a training manual?"

"No, a handbook. She told me to study it if I wanted to stay on the team." Hannah cleared her throat. "Only, it doesn't seem to be a normal kind of book."

"Can we look at it?" Alicia asked.

"Yeah, I'll go get it." Hannah rose from the table and retrieved her handbag from the entryway. She could already feel the book pulsing from within, begging for her to touch it, begging to be opened. She had resisted cracking open the cover up until that moment, but now, among new friends, it felt safer somehow. She sat back down, pulled the thick black book from her bag, and set it on the table.

"Whoa." Alicia held up her hands and backed away. "That book has major bad vibes."

Hector's eyes darted from Alicia to Hannah. "Can I see that?"

"Yeah." Hannah passed the book across the table.

Hector readjusted his glasses and opened the cover of the book. He pursed his lips and frowned as he flipped the pages. "Babe, you should take a look at this."

"Mmm- mmm. *No way.*" Alicia hugged herself and rubbed the back of her arms. "I'm not touching it."

Hector glanced back at Hannah. "I don't think you should read this."

"Why?"

"Because you'll die, that's why."

"I'll die? From a book?" Hannah's eyebrows met as she gave him a frown of disbelief. "How can a book hurt me?"

"See these symbols? My grandma always told me never to mess with that stuff." Hector shook his head and handed the book back to her. "Seriously. You could get hurt."

"They're just symbols." Prickles of electricity shot up and down Hannah's arms as she grasped the handbook.

She opened the cover and stared at the contents inside, her eyes glazing over the page. The entire book was written in a language that she didn't recognize, but the longer she stared at the page, the more the symbols began to make sense. A high-pitched ringing pierced through her ears, the scent of decay and flowers filled her nostrils, and a metallic taste coated her tongue.

"Hector and I took an Occult in Media class as part of our undergrad art program," Alicia said. "Remember the Suwannee Cannibal?"

Hannah glanced over at Alicia and shuddered. "Yeah. He killed a bunch of college students in the eighties and nineties, right?"

"Killed and *ate* them. He had that written all over the walls of his apartment." Hector pointed to the symbol at the top of the first page. "When they finally caught the guy, he claimed to be some kind of demon."

The icon was a strange blend of ouroboros and pentagram that seemed almost familiar to her. The longer and closer she looked, the more the image seemed to shift and writhe on the page. Hannah's forehead slickened with sweat, and her breath came in sharp and fast as a low growl emanated from within the pages.

She slammed the cover shut. "What the hell!"

"See? You don't want to mess with that," Hector said, his gaze darting back to Alicia.

Alicia rose from her seat and hurried to the kitchen. She opened a kitchen drawer, pulled out a bundle of wrapped leaves, lit one end with a match, and began to wave it in the air.

She shook her head and stared at Hannah through the smoke with a look of concern. "Sorry, but you have to get that book out of here."

Hannah shoved the book back into her bag and wiped her forehead with the back of her hand. Her heart was still beating like a trapped butterfly.

Deep down, she knew what Hector was saying was right. That the handbook was all wrong. *Dangerous*, even. Still, the energy that flowed through her when she opened the cover, the way it felt so good in her hand. She had to admit, it felt… *right*.

"Sorry if I ruined your dinner. I'll see you at work tomorrow, I guess." Hannah stood on wobbly ankles and rushed to the door with her body on fire. She slipped into her flats and was surprised as a fat, salty tear rolled down her cheek. She wiped it away and a loud chuckle exploded from her chest.

"Hannah, wait!"

Hector placed a hand on her shoulder. She turned to face him and he gasped and pulled his hand away.

"It's okay." She smiled, her pulse leveling out. "Everything is going to be fine."

"Hannah, don't read that book," he said and opened his front door. "Seriously."

"I won't," she said. "Goodnight."

"Good night."

With that, Hannah slipped out of the safety of Hector and Alicia's apartment into the muggy evening air. Her handbag banged at her side as she descended the stairs, and the book beckoned her to open it again as she passed the bright lights and bustle of downtown Tampa at night. The neon lights burned bright, leaving smudge trails and a kaleidoscope of color in her line of sight. The laughter of a couple passing by blasted in her ear and traffic roared past her in a deafening wave. The humidity pressed down upon her, wrapping her in a hot, wet hug as her feet pounded on the sidewalk. The urge to take the book out again followed her all the way back to the hotel. She wanted to feel its smooth cover in her hands, to sniff the pages and caress them like a lover. She wanted the book and the book wanted her.

Hannah reached her hotel room, flung her handbag on the dresser, and collapsed in an exhausted heap on the bed. The downy white coverlet had been pulled tight by the housekeeping staff, creating a tautt, military precision surface. She closed her eyes waiting for her heart to slow down to a normal pace and thought about home. Part of her wanted to go back and try to connect with her family and community again, especially when things got tough or lonely. The feelings of isolation, unworthiness, and fear were going to be with her no matter where she called home unless she could figure out how to live with herself. Part of her never wanted to return home, even if she hadn't been cast out. From the moment she was little, the elders in her community knew her true nature and only tolerated her for as long as they had to. The congregation made it known to her that she wasn't one of them all her life, constantly reinforcing that she was tainted somehow—that she was *bad*. But that small voice that whispered to her always told her that she was meant for bigger things. Every step she had made up to now pointed her to this place and this time. To *Visage*.

Just as she was beginning to relax, the ringing in her ears returned, followed by the overwhelming aroma of roses and a copper penny flavor in her mouth. Sharp claws of hunger raked through her stomach. She rolled to her side in the fetal position, clutching her abdomen. Her head began to spin with vertigo as she forced herself to sit upright. The air pressure in the room seemed to change, and Hannah realized something was very wrong.

And then, something sat next to her on the bed. The side of the pristine, perfectly made bed that Hannah hadn't touched was dented in the shape of a person. A very large, very heavy person. She covered her mouth in a silent scream and scrambled to her feet, her pulse and breathing elevated. Hannah stared at the impression on the pristine coverlet and let out a shuddered breath of frost into the air. The hair on her forearms stood as a low, clicking sound buzzed through the air and the impression released itself from the bed.

Hannah slowly backed up against the dresser, refusing to take her eyes off the bed. The book called out to her again from inside her handbag. It tugged at her breast. She needed to get rid of it. She grabbed her bag and backed out of the hotel room, eyes still fixed to the spot where something definitely had just been sitting. There was no way she would be able to return to that room and sleep there. She ran out of her room, through the hotel lobby, and into the night. The book was clearly evil, but there was no way in hell that Hannah would step foot on sacred ground. So she headed instinctively towards the only place that she could consider getting rid of a cursed object.

The Hillsborough River ran through downtown Tampa along a park bustling with people and nightlife, meaning she would have no privacy for her deed. Hannah ran past laughing college students, a bachelorette party, and a family out for an evening stroll. Despite the crowd, no one seemed to take notice of her. She ran until a stitch formed in her side and the brackish water of the river filled her senses. She gasped and held onto the railing overlooking the dark water, the book still crying out to her from her bag. Deep down, Hannah knew that the book wanted her, and a dark, horrible part of her wanted the book, too. It wanted her to read its cursed contents, to let it consume her mind, body, and soul. She couldn't let it. She plunged her hand into her bag and felt the glorious, horrible volume in her palm once more. Without another thought, she flung the book into the river and cackled.

The ringing had stopped. The strange smell and taste had stopped. Hannah began her trek back to the hotel, cautiously optimistic that whatever was happening with the handbook was over. As she strolled through the park bathed in moonlight, she made a plan. She knew that she couldn't stay at *Visage* any longer, but she couldn't go home either. Running away again wasn't an option.

For now, Hannah still needed a place to stay. She would ride out her internship at *Visage* and enjoy her free hotel room as long as she could stand it, but one thing was for sure: she couldn't stay in *that* room one second longer. She put on her best, most trustworthy expression as she approached the concierge desk of the hotel. She said a silent prayer that she didn't appear as hectic on the outside as she felt on the inside. She cleared her throat and for a moment, tasted something briny and earthy. The attendant glanced her way in recognition.

Hannah coughed, shook her head, and smiled. "I'd like to see if I could switch my room for the night, please."

CHAPTER SIX

Hannah slept like the dead in her new hotel room. With the help of the hotel staff, all of her meager belongings were moved to a different room without issue. There was no sense of dread, no strange sounds, smells, or sensations in the new room—just the comfort and ease that she always sought out in life. Clean towels. Endless cable television. A climate controlled room just for her. Shelter and food security would be hard to let go of when her time at *Visage* came to an end.

Though it was only the third day of Hannah's internship, she had already experienced a lifetime's worth of tension and anxiety on the job. She was starting to understand why the intern before her didn't stick around. Any normal person would have quit, but Hannah wasn't any normal person. She had already been to hell and back, and a few office bullies and a weird book weren't going to scare her away just yet. Without the *Visage* internship she would be on the street again, and that was a life Hannah was determined never to go back to.

"Hey." Hector grimaced and lowered his headphones as she entered their cubicle that morning. "How's it going?"

"Good morning," Hannah said and flopped down in her seat. "I'm fine. Sorry that dinner got so... *weird* last night."

"It's okay." Hector's upper lip twitched as he glanced at her bag. "What did you do with the handbook?"

"Tossed it in the Hillsborough River." Hannah shrugged. "You're right. There was something fucked up about that book."

"What are you going to tell Grace?" he whispered.

"About what?"

"When she asks about the book?" Hector swiveled around and glanced out into the hallway. "What are you going to tell her?"

"I'm not going to tell her anything," Hannah said, "I'm going to spend the rest of the week applying for every possible job I can find. I'll fly under the radar until I have a new job and then I'm out of here."

"What if she asks you about the book?"

"I'll just lie and say that I'm reading it," she answered.

"*Okay.*" He pulled a face and grabbed his headphones.

"Hector, there's one more thing." Hannah bit her lower lip and thought back to the incident on her bed the night before. The feeling of being cold, the strange smells and sensations. She wanted to tell Hector all about it. She also didn't want her only friend in town to think she was absolutely bonkers.

Still, the memory of feeling like something was in the room with her left her feeling haunted. The fact that she couldn't allow herself to tell anyone made her feel more alone than ever.

"What?"

"Never mind. It's nothing." Hannah sighed and logged onto her computer. An email from Valerie requesting another coffee pickup for the morning meeting sat in her queue, glaring at her. She frowned and deleted the email. Anton had never paid her back for the first coffee run. She wasn't about to get screwed again. There was also an email from Grace stating that the office would be closed on Thursday and Friday for the long holiday weekend. Hannah had been so wrapped up in everything that had been going on that she had forgotten all about the upcoming Fourth of July holiday. That email sent a wave of relief through her body; this little break would give her even more time to go job hunting on *Visage's* dime.

Caught up on her inbox, Hannah stretched and glanced out into the hallway. The Corporate Coven had congregated in the hallway, their heads together and hands flying wildly. Hannah snorted and watched their heated discussion from a distance. Ice flowed through her veins as their heads snapped around in unison and three pairs of eyes stared directly at her.

She sucked in a sharp breath through her nose and turned her gaze back to her screen. It was nearly time for the morning meeting, and she dreaded the prospect of having to be in the same room with any of them again. She pulled out her makeup bag, checked her reflection, and steeled herself for what was sure to be an uncomfortable half hour. Hannah held her head high as she entered Grace's darkened office that morning. She could already sense the weight of their stares as she took her seat. She pursed her lips and propped her hands in her lap, ready for whatever venom they wanted to spew her way. She could take it.

"Hannah, where's our coffee order?" Valerie's sing-song voice floated across the room. She smiled, her lips frosted in a champagne pink lip gloss that matched her prom-style party dress. Between her poofy sleeves and cascade of curls, Valerie looked more like a princess that someone would hire for a children's party than an office worker.

"I won't be fetching coffee or lunch orders anymore." Hannah cleared her throat and sat up straight. "Anton hasn't paid me back yet. Besides, It's not my job."

"*Oooh*," Fox chortled from behind a gloved hand.

"She's right." Grace stood over her desk with her palms placed flat on the surface. "Hannah is reading the handbook."

"Seriously?" Valerie scoffed. Her lower lip quivered and hung open wide. "But she's…."

"Quit sniveling," Grace barked.

Selena chuckled to herself and shifted in her seat. Her black leatherette leggings squeaked as she crossed her legs.

Grace pierced Selena with a look. "Do you have anything you would like to say?"

"No, ma'am," Selena half laughed.

"We have a long holiday weekend, so I trust you're all caught up with your assignments," Grace continued, "but in light of the newest member of our staff joining us, I have a new assignment for you this weekend. Hannah, I need you to join the team scouting for models tomorrow night."

Hannah's brow furrowed as her gaze darted from Selena to Fox and Valerie and then back to Grace again. "Model scouting?"

"Yes. We have a special feature planned for the new year. Going forward, *Visage* is going to be focusing more on street style, and that means we'll need real people. Real models." Grace sat and grazed her fingertips along the collar of her jewel-embellished neckline. "Bring Hector with you to take some headshots for reference."

"I'm sorry, but, at night?" Hannah glanced around the room.

The senior writers looked as thrilled as she did at the prospect of spending time with her outside of the office.

"Yes. Your contract states that you must make yourself available for special events. This falls under that." Grace adjusted her glasses to look down her nose at her writers.

"Now, can I trust you all to play nice?"

"Yes ma'am," the writers all said in unison.

"That'll be all. Hannah, stay back a moment. I need to speak with you."

Hannah's eyes grew wide as the writers stood and brushed past her out into the hall. She smoothed down the hem of her plain black dress and approached Grace's desk.

Grace scribbled across a page with a fountain pen in long, artful loops. "You've been reading the handbook, yes?"

"Uh, yes ma'am."

"And what do you think?" Grace looked up at her with a pensive stare.

"I think it's... very interesting."

"Good." Grace smiled, folded the paper and held it toward her. "This is the name and address of my hairdresser, Jean, as well as my contact at Rodanthe House across the street. Tomorrow, on your day off, I'd like you to go treat yourself to a fresh haircut and some new clothes."

"Oh." Hannah blinked and accepted the paper. "Ma'am I don't think I...."

"Anton will give you the company card," Grace said, waving her off. "Don't worry about the expense. If you're going to be part of the team, I want you to look like it."

"Okay. Thank you." Hannah held her breath for a moment and then turned toward the door.

"Oh, and one more thing."

Hannah turned back to see Grace staring at her, hands folded on the desk in front of her.

"Be sure to *really* study that handbook."

"I will, ma'am."

Hannah let out a low, shuddery breath as she emerged into the hallway. Valerie, Fox, and Selena were waiting for her, as she had expected they would be. None of them looked pleased.

"So, it sounds like you'll be joining us on our girls' night out tomorrow." Valerie spread a faux, sickly sweet smile across her lips and approached her.

"Yeah." Hannah clutched the paper that Grace had given her to her chest. "Hector is coming, too."

"Oh, right." Selena's eyes flashed as she approached, her gaze set on Hannah's paper. "What's that?"

"Grace is sending me to her hairdresser," Hannah said, "and to some place called Rodanthe House."

"Of course she is." Valerie pouted and placed her hand on top of Hannah's head. She stroked the length of her long dark hair and plucked out a single strand.

"Ow!" Hannah jerked back.

"Meet us at Ultra Lounge tomorrow night at ten." Fox tugged at Valerie's arm. "And don't forget to wear something decent."

The senior writers turned their back on her and moved toward their respective offices.

"Wait!" she shouted. "Where's Ultra Lounge?"

Hannah let out an exasperated breath and returned to the shared office space. Hector was busy at his desk editing the lingerie photo shoot from the day before. The memory of how Selena had treated her and the model sent a fresh dose of rage seething through her veins.

He turned as she sat down at her desk and lowered his headphones. "So how'd it go?"

"It went… fine? Weird? I don't know." Hannah glanced down at the paper. "Did you know we have to go to this thing tomorrow night?"

"Yeah. The talent scout thing," Hector scoffed. "I'll probably bring Alicia."

"Cool." She held up the paper. "Grace is paying for me to get my hair done and get some clothes tomorrow. Is this something she usually does?"

"Ah. The indoctrination." Hector nodded.

"What's that mean?"

"Well, Jenn went and got her hair done a few days after they hired her, too." Hector stretched in his seat.

"The intern who was here before me?"

"Yeah. Come to think of it, she stopped talking to me after that." Hector scratched his head. "I just hope that doesn't happen to you too."

"I don't know if I'm going to get a haircut or not." Hannah took out her compact mirror and regarded her complexion. Her long, dark hair fell in pin-straight swaths to the center of her back. It was the same bland and basic hairstyle she'd had since she was a child. "I wouldn't mind some new clothes, though."

"Oh, you got a package by the way." Hector reached across his desk, retrieved a padded manila envelope and handed it to her. "Here."

"Are you sure it's for me?" Hannah reluctantly accepted the package.

No one would have known she was there, except perhaps her former college professor. She hadn't told anyone her whereabouts, and she didn't know anyone in town outside of her co-workers at *Visage Magazine* and the hotel staff. The front of the package was clearly addressed to her in a hand that she didn't recognize.

"I don't know any other Hannah Howarths." Hector shrugged.

Hannah ripped open the package, but before she had even pulled out the contents, she knew what was inside. Her mouth filled with the taste of sulfurous, salty water and a dull ringing settled in between her ears. She held her breath and pulled out a wet, black book from inside the envelope. Her hand shook as she held up the cursed handbook..

"Hector," she gasped, "it's back."

The book made a squidgy sound and yelped as it wriggled in her hands.

Hannah screeched and tossed the book on the floor.

"I thought you threw that thing into the river?" He blinked and readjusted his glasses.

"I did!"

Hector recoiled. "Well how did it get back here?"

"I don't know!" Hannah pulled out a filing cabinet drawer on the side of her desk, her heart pounding. She grabbed her cardigan and used it to wrap up the book. She tossed the book, cardigan and all, inside the filing cabinet and secured the lock at the top.

"There." She pulled out the key and turned back to Hector.

"Did someone see you throw the book away?"

"I don't think so." She shook her head. "This is too weird."

"What are you gonna do?"

"I don't know." Hannah's hands were still damp with river water. Her stomach lurched as she wiped her hands on her skirt. "I have to get out of here. I'm going to go home sick."

"Okay." Hector glanced at the filing cabinet with a worried look. "Are you going to be all right?"

"Yeah. I think so." Hannah typed off an email to Grace and the team and picked up her bag. "I'll see you tomorrow night, I guess."

"Sure. Go get some rest."

"Thanks." She picked up her bag and hurried down the hallway without looking back.

Anton glared at her with a questioning look as she moved toward the elevator. "Going somewhere?"

"Yes. I'm not feeling well. I'm going home sick."

"Grace asked me to give you this." Anton held out a black plastic card in her direction. "She said she expects you to use it."

Hannah plucked the credit card from his hand

and examined it. A whole new world of possibilities coursed through her as she stared at the slim, plastic rectangle. She could rent a car and drive far, far away. She could buy a month's worth of supplies and disappear into the woods. She could start a whole new life all over again. Still, she wasn't ready to leave Tampa and her life as Hannah Howarth behind just yet.

"Thanks." Hannah turned and entered the elevator. Her long holiday weekend was off to an early start.

CHAPTER SEVEN

"*Voilà.* You're a whole new woman."

Hannah opened her eyes, gazed back at her reflection, and gasped. Thick, blunt bangs swept across her forehead highlighting her dark eyes and high cheekbones. She tilted her head to appreciate the way her new bob just grazed the top of her collarbone. Jean was right. She *was* a new woman.

"Give Grace my love, won't you?" Jean gently lifted the smock from her shoulders and brushed away a strand of dark hair. "She's due for a refresh soon."

"I will. Thank you." Hannah stood in her newly acquired black silk jumpsuit from Rodanthe House. A few swipes of lipstick and mascara and her transformation would be complete. She had never considered herself to be vain before, but she couldn't stop looking at herself. She felt refreshed. *Powerful.*

The sun was setting outside the salon as Hannah paid for her cut and color with the *Visage* corporate card. Her eyes bugged a little as she looked at the total, but she didn't think twice about giving Jean a generous tip. Her wardrobe from Rodanthe House had been pricey too, though Celine the stylist there, had explained to Hannah that it was all considered a business expense that Grace could write off. Hannah's stomach rumbled and the credit card burned hot in her hand. Certainly, the accounting department wouldn't notice a sushi roll added to the long list of charges.

Instead of walking and ruining her new ensemble, Hannah used the corporate card to pay for a cab to Ybor City. She was dropped off in front of Blue Wave Sushi, just a half block from Ultra Lounge as the nightlife began to pick up. She walked into the restaurant and could feel the weight of a dozen stares as she slipped into a booth. For so long she had simply tried to blend in with the crowd, to stay in the background and out of the spotlight. Now with her new look, people were practically compelled to look.

Hannah sat in the booth and ate her sushi slowly and with purpose, relishing every moment. She looked transformed. She *felt* transformed. The sensation of black satin against her skin, the elegant feel of chopsticks between her fingers, the way it felt for men and women alike to stare at her and want her. It was all so new. If this was what it was like to be drunk on power, Hannah was in danger of becoming addicted.

By nine thirty, Hannah had finished her dinner, but she hadn't received a text from Hector. He and Alicia were supposed to be on their way to the nightclub soon to begin passing out release forms and taking photos. As Hannah walked up to the venue, she could see why Grace had ordered her and the Corporate Coven to go there—lined up on the sidewalk were the most beautiful, unique looking people waiting to get in. There were punks with liberty spikes, goths in fishnets, preppy college kids with popped collars, Botox babes in bodycon dresses, men with mullets and mustaches, women with expertly crafted club ensembles. Every conceivable type of young, fashionable scenester was waiting to get into Ultra. This was a place to see and be seen.

"Well, looks like Jean worked his magic again." A pale, thin arm slipped through Hannah's, snapping her from her haze. "Celine isn't very original though. She gave me the same damn jumpsuit."

A dagger-like manicure wrapped around her other arm, and Hannah recoiled. "Hey! Hands off!"

Valerie and Selena cackled in unison as they dragged her to the front of the line. Selena was dressed in a strappy sequined mini dress, her hair piled on top of her head. Valerie was wearing a flower print vintage shift dress with her hair teased into a bouffant. Hannah snapped her head around to see Fox walking behind them, smoking a long, slim cigarette and wearing a Cramps T-shirt under a boxy, black blazer.

"Don't be so uptight, Hannah." Valerie hugged her arm and leaned her head on her shoulder. "The bouncer won't think you're cool and then you'll have to go to the back of the line."

Hannah pursed her lips as Selena greeted the bouncer at the front of the line. The man nodded and moved the velvet rope aside, allowing them to cut the long line. Nineties techno music and a blast of frigid air greeted them as they stepped over the threshold into the darkened night club and bellied up to the bar.

"Where's the card?" Valerie turned to Hannah and held out her hand with her palm facing up. She tapped her palm with her index finger and raised her eyebrows. "Hand it over."

"What card?" Hannah asked.

"The corporate credit card, genius." Selena sneered. "We know Grace gave it to you."

"I... I left it back at my hotel room," Hannah lied.

"Great." Fox huffed.

"Fine." Valerie blew out a frustrated breath between her frosted lips. "Selena, it's your turn to get drinks then."

Selena's eyes flash. "Of *course*. I always have to."

"You always have to *what*?" Valerie scowled, nostrils flaring. The two were locked in a death match of glares, lips curled and claws extended like apex predators ready to pounce. Hannah froze and held her breath, part of her smugly enjoying watching her two co-workers go at each other's throats. Another part of her was just terrified.

"Nothing." Selena backed down.

The bartender greeted them and Selena

ordered four drinks. She winked at the bartender and Hannah could swear she heard the bartender say, "on the house." Selena pushed a glass into her hand and gave drinks to Fox and Valerie as well.

"I don't drink," Hannah said.

"You do tonight," Valerie snickered. "Come on. Consider this a team-building exercise."

"Look, Fox. Over there." Selena tilted her chin across the dance floor. The nightclub was beginning to fill up with all of the beautiful people who had been standing outside. A woman with cropped dark hair stood against a wall with her hands in her jean pockets looking uncomfortable and alone.

"Go make a friend." Selena shoved Fox's shoulder in the woman's direction.

Fox popped the collar of their blazer. "I intend to."

"Well, I see *my* friend for the night." Selena downed the rest of her drink, readjusted her bra straps, and smoothed a strand of loose hair. "Bye, bitches."

Hannah gripped her icy beverage and watched as Selena plunked her empty glass on the counter and made her way toward a man on the other side of the bar. Her target was tall and muscular with the look of a professional athlete. His features bloomed and brightened as Selena approached him and led him to the dance floor.

"What is going on?" Hannah turned to Valerie and shook her head. "Aren't we supposed to be scouting for models?"

"We *are*." Valerie slowly sipped her drink, her eyes scanning the crowd. She smiled, grabbed Hannah's arm, and squeezed. "There. That's your guy."

She followed Valerie's line of sight toward a couch in the corner of the room. A man about her age with dark hair and glasses in a white-button down sat alone, scrolling through his phone.

Hannah glanced over at Valerie, who met her gaze with a wolfish grin. "My guy for what?" Hannah asked.

Valerie rolled her eyes. "Go *charm* him. You've been reading the handbook, right?"

"I have. Only just a little." Hannah winced, lying again.

"Great. So get him to ask you to dance," Valerie said. "You look hot. It should be easy enough."

"I'm not interested in dancing with anyone. I just want to wait for Hector."

"Hector isn't coming," Valerie laughed.

"What? Who's going to take photos then?"

Valerie shrugged. "Guess we don't need them."

"But what about model scouting?" Hannah reached for her handbag. A quick text to Hector would clear all this up. "Aren't we supposed to be recruiting new street style models?"

"This is all part of the deal. Trust me." Valerie grabbed Hannah's hands. "Come on, now. You don't want to disappoint Grace. Get one of these dumb dumbs to dance with you."

Hannah hugged her arms to her chest. "How

do I do it?"

"*Ugh*. It's easy." Valerie grabbed her shoulders and turned Hannah to face her. She locked eyes with her and puffed out her lips. "You just gaze into their eyes and, like, tell them to look at you with your mind."

"That's ridiculous," Hannah snickered, but couldn't pull away from Valerie's gaze.

Valerie's pink frosted lips curled up into a wicked grin, and her voice echoed through Hannah's mind. *Not so ridiculous now, is it?*

"*Shit*," Hannah gasped and pulled away.

Valerie snort-laughed, "See? Piece of cake."

Hannah glanced back over across the dance floor. Selena and the jock were grinding on each other to a fast electronic song and Fox and the shy woman were making out in a dark corner. The sea of bodies parted and the man with the glasses looked up from his phone and stared directly at her.

"Now, just use your thoughts to influence him," Valerie said. "Try it."

Hannah licked her lips. *Come over here.*

The man stood, put his phone in his pocket, and began to walk her way.

"Holy shit."

"Told ya." Valerie shrugged and patted her shoulder. "I've got my eyes on that long-haired pretty boy over there. Have fun."

Hannah placed her still-full glass on the bar as Valerie disappeared into the crowd. She smoothed out her new bob, and tried on a smile as the bespectacled man approached her.

"Hey," he said, "can I buy you a beer?"

"I already have a drink." Hannah motioned to her glass. Then the next thing that flew out of her mouth truly surprised her. "Wanna dance instead?"

"Definitely."

Hannah grabbed the man's hand and pulled him into the sea of bodies. She had never been to a nightclub before and didn't even recognize most of the music. She didn't know how to dance or act around someone, and had only been on a few disastrous dates up to that point. However, with her new look, Hannah had become a new person. She tilted her head back as the music flowed through her and stared at the colorful lights until they burned her eyes. She gave into the wave of the crowd and let something else take over. She wasn't Hannah anymore. She was becoming something else. Something shiny and perfect and new. She was becoming something better.

CHAPTER EIGHT

"Fox. Call a cab." Selena threw Valerie a dirty look as she bummed a cigarette from Fox. It was just after two a.m. and Ultra was closing for the night. The tired, beautiful people of Ybor City were all heading home, but for the Corporate Coven, the night had just begun. Selena's new athletic boyfriend was at her side, swallowing her body inside his massive, beefy arms. Fox's shy new friend was also in tow with her head down and her face buried in her phone. Hannah glanced at her own bespectacled date for the night and realized she didn't even know his name.

"Are we going back to your place this time?" Fox scowled, pulling out a cell phone and tapping away at the screen.

"Of course. Hannah, what's your friend's name?" Valerie clung on to the arm of a man with long, dark hair and soulful eyes.

"Oh, I don't... what *is* your name?" Hannah glanced at the man at her side under the harsh street lights.

"Jeremy." He glanced down at the sidewalk, blushing.

"Well, *Jeremy*. Would you like to come back

to my place for a drink?" Valerie asked. "I only live about five minutes away."

"Sure." He shrugged and glanced over at Hannah from behind his frames.

A twinge of guilt settled in as Hannah wore an awkward smile. Jeremy seemed to be shy and sweet, but she didn't want anything to do with him. As she stood on the sidewalk, the buzz of the nightclub began to wear off, and all Hannah wanted to do was go back to the hotel, book a bus ticket to wherever on the *Visage* corporate card, and disappear. Something about the look in Valerie's eye told her that leaving the group wasn't an option.

"Valerie, I'm worn out. If we're finished "model scouting" I'm going back to my hotel."

"You can't leave." Valerie's eyes flashed. "You're one of us now."

"No, actually, I'm not. I'm done."

"Too late." Valerie grinned as a minivan pulled up to the curb.

Hannah sighed and obeyed as the group piled into the cab. She was caught in their magnetic pull, and even though her gut and that small voice inside her said not to go with them, she went anyway. In the past, she had always let everyone tell her what to do, where to go. The new Hannah was supposed to be independent. Stronger. So far, the new Hannah was failing.

Jeremy pressed up against her in the minivan and tried to hold her hand as they drove through Ybor City and back toward downtown Tampa. The

Corporate Coven threw their heads back and cackled at one another as their acquired dates for the night sat silently by their sides like obedient dogs. After only a few minutes of driving, Hannah was surprised when the cab stopped only a block away from Tampa Towers.

One-by-one, the crew spilled out of the van into the night and followed Valerie into the lobby of her building. They all filed into the elevator, and Valerie pressed the button for the top floor. The penthouse.

The elevator doors opened onto a grand foyer outfitted with marble floors, glass sconces, and gilded accents. There were only two entryways on the top floor; Valerie veered to the right, pulled out her keys, and let her guests in. The luxury apartment was dark, save for a strip of neon lights over a bar area along the back wall. The floors were made of polished black marble, and two black sectional sofas were the only furniture in the open floor plan. Hannah's mouth hung open as she surveyed the dark, dimly-lit space and its panoramic view of the city and Tampa Bay. The apartment was far too luxurious for a magazine staff writer to be able to afford.

"So, is this your parents' apartment or something?" Hannah eyed a painting in the entryway. The gray and black abstract composition looked suspiciously similar to the painting hanging over Grace's office.

"Something like that," Valerie snorted. "Who

wants a drink?"

Fox slid behind the bar at the far end of the living room and pulled out a bottle and a stack of glasses. Selena and her new friend sunk down onto one of the couches overlooking the city while Valerie disappeared into a bedroom with the long-haired man. Hannah's date stood in a daze just staring out the window.

"It feels so safe." Jeremy's voice was slow and dreamy. "Just like when I was little. My mom would wrap me in a towel after a long day of swimming. I would have lunch and fall asleep in her lap without even knowing I fell asleep."

"What are you talking about?" Hannah shook her head and glanced around the room.

"It's like being wrapped in a cocoon. Falling back into a dark, comfortable place where nothing can hurt me."

Jeremy closed his eyes and swayed on his feet. Hannah's breath hitched as that same sensation she had felt in Grace's office overwhelmed her. It was as if she was standing at the edge of a cliff and something was at her back threatening to push her over. She didn't feel safe. Despite her sushi dinner feast and the strange atmosphere, Hannah was starting to feel hungry. She followed Jeremy's line of sight out of the window toward the illuminated Tampa skyline as it glittered all around them. Something large and dark whooshed by the window, with wings flapping like some great bird. She gasped and her shoulders tensed. Her stomach dropped and she steadied herself.

"Jeremy, I...."

A muffled scream floated through Valerie's closed bedroom door, followed by a loud thud. Fox turned on a television mounted to the wall and clicked to a music channel with loud techno and continued to make out with the shy, short-haired girl. Selena's date had disappeared somewhere underneath her on the couch as she writhed on top of him. Hannah's stomach knotted and a sick spurt of acidic bile filled her mouth as she surveyed the scene. Something was *wrong*.

"We have to get out of here," she whispered and grabbed Jeremy's hand. His fingers were cold and limp in her hand. She tugged at his arm, but he didn't budge.

"Jeremy! We need to go," Hannah hissed. "Come on!"

Before Hannah had a chance to make her move, Valerie's bedroom door flung open with exaggerated force. Hannah gasped and all of the feeling left her body as her co-worker stood before her in the doorway, naked, her mouth wet with red. It wasn't Valerie's nudity or the abrupt opening of the door that caused Hannah to choke back a scream. Great, black, leathery wings had sprouted at Valerie's shoulder blades and her eyes glowed highlighter green in the dark. But her *mouth*. Her mouth was the most terrifying of all.

Valerie's maw opened wide and a guttural laugh escaped through rows of razor sharp teeth.

"What's the matter, Hannah? Can't hang?"

Hannah's breath caught in her throat and she began to back away. She tugged at Jeremy's hand again but he remained cemented in place, his eyes fixed on the window. The shy woman squelched and wiggled on the couch as Fox's jaw unhinged and sank a row of sharp teeth into her throat. Selena's head popped up from the other side of the couch and she glared at Hannah with two glowing green eyes. Selena spread out her own set of velvety black wings as the meat and sinews of the athletic man clung from her chin, staining the front of her sequined dress. Hannah stumbled and she willed her numb legs to move faster as she backed into the door.

"We were just starting to have fun!" Valerie unhinged her jaw again with the wet sound of ripping flesh. The creature screamed, the sound bouncing off the walls of the apartment, sending shockwaves through Hannah's body. She moved toward a petrified Jeremy, who was quiet and still as a scared prey animal in headlights.

Hannah's hand closed around the doorknob, and she could only watch as Jeremy's head disappeared into Valerie's open maw, glasses and all. Red spurted in great arcs from the open neckhole of the now headless body in an almost comical manner, not unlike a fountain. A hot droplet of blood hit Hannah's cheek as she flung the door open. She ran to the elevator and slammed the button to close the doors, her pulse jackhammering inside her skull. The doors closed torturously slow, and

Hannah almost expected the trio of ghouls to appear and drag her back into the apartment from hell.

She bolted from the elevator as soon as the doors opened on the ground floor, refusing to look back. Nothing that she had just witnessed made sense and terror was the only emotion propelling her forward. She didn't know what to make of the scene that she had just witnessed, only that she knew it was very real and very fucked up. She ran past her hotel with her lungs on fire and her heart threatening to beat out of her chest, and it dawned on her then what must have happened to the other intern. She couldn't go back to her hotel room. They would know where to find her. Instead, Hannah headed to the only other place in town that she knew.

❋ ❋ ❋

"Hector! Hector, open up!" Hannah pounded on the apartment door with a closed fist and a scream trapped in her lungs. It was nearly three a.m., and showing up at his place at that time of night was decidedly not a cool thing to do. But Hector was the only person who would understand. He was the only one who would possibly believe her. If she could even believe what she saw herself, that was.

"Hannah! Jesus!" Hector opened the door and squinted. He was dressed in a t-shirt that said "Han Shot First" with a pair of Star Wars pajama pants, his hair ruffled in a tangle of curls. He sleepily put on his glasses as he closed the door behind her.

"They're *monsters*! They're fucking monsters!" Hannah panted and leaned against the wall. Her legs turned to jelly. She needed to sit.

"What happened? Is she okay?" Alicia appeared dressed in a long nightgown, her hair in a messy bun. "Wait. Hannah, are you bleeding?"

Hannah shook her head and closed her eyes. "It's not my blood."

"I'm gonna get you a glass of water." Alicia exchanged a worried look with Hector and disappeared into the kitchen.

"I'm really sorry to barge in on you like this," Hannah said as Hector helped her to her feet. "I just... I don't know where else to go."

"What happened?"

Hannah sat down at the dining table where they had shared tacos only a few nights ago and attempted to organize her thoughts. Everything she was about to say would come out sounding insane. Alicia gave her a glass of water and she downed it, taking her time to try and calm her nerves. She placed the empty glass on the table, took in a deep breath, and glanced at Hector and Alicia.

"I don't know how else to say this. Selena, Valerie, Fox... they're monsters. They eat people."

Hector's gaze flicked to Alicia, then back to Hannah again. "I'm sorry. What?"

"Valerie, Selena, and Fox are monsters. Like not just socially. Like, for really real. They had fucking *bat wings*." Hannah snorted at herself in disbelief and covered her mouth with her hands. "They *ate* them."

"Hold up, hold up," Hector laughed. "You can't be serious."

"I wish I wasn't. We all brought dates back to Valerie's apartment. She lives in this super fancy place. I thought they were going to just keep drinking or get high or something. Instead, it was a fucking *bloodbath*."

"Maybe we should take you to the emergency room?" Hector frowned.

"No," she said. "I'm not hurt, just shook up."

Hector folded his hands together on the table. "Are you sure they didn't slip you something in your drink?"

She shook her head. "I didn't drink anything. It sounds insane, but I know what I saw."

"I want to believe you, it just sounds so… *unreal*." Hector scratched the back of his neck. "I'm sorry we weren't there tonight. Alicia wasn't feeling well, so we stayed home."

"Don't apologize. It's a good thing you stayed home." Hannah rapped her fingertips on the table, her blood beginning to boil. "The whole model scouting thing was a scam. They weren't working. They were *hunting*."

"So, the people you met at the bar," Hector said, "you're sure they're dead?"

"Valerie ate my date's head." Hannah blinked. "He seemed like such a nice guy too. Jeremy."

"She's covered in blood. Clearly *something* happened." Alicia held up her phone. "Should we call the cops?"

"I thought about that, but the police won't believe me anyway." Hannah pressed her hands together. "This is a lot to ask, but can I please stay here tonight?"

Hector glanced at Alicia with a worried expression. The thought of the ghouls bursting through Hector's front door and ripping him and Alicia to pieces flashed before her eyes. It was a mistake to come to her only friends in town. She would never forgive herself for putting them in danger too.

"You know what, on second thought, they might come looking for me here." Hannah stood and grabbed her bag. "I'm sorry I barged in on you. I shouldn't involve you."

"Wait! I don't think you should...."

"Hector, whatever you do, don't go back to the office." Hannah bolted toward the door as a new burst of adrenaline flooded her veins.

She didn't wait to hear Hector's pleas as she vanished again into the night. She was scared and alone in a strange town where she knew no one and nothing felt safe. Cloaked in the dark, sweltering hours of early morning, Hannah faded away into the shadows as she had done before. As she was destined to do once again.

CHAPTER NINE

Hannah sat at the end of a farmhouse dinner table with a fork in one hand, a knife in the other, and a napkin tucked into her shirt. Her nose twitched at the familiar scent of laundry detergent and the deep-set mold that lived within the walls of her family home. She was cast aside at the end of the table again, and it was supper time.

She glanced up at the dining room wall and spotted the collage of photos hanging over the credenza, all twelve of her siblings in descending order and then her, the baby. The family photo at the center of it all showed her stair step siblings, each a year apart and dressed similarly, the boys in white polo shirts and jeans, the girls in conservative floral dresses with high necks and long sleeves. Dad still had a little hair left back then and wore his signature thick lens, plastic frame glasses. Mom's permed hair and wavy bangs were sprayed high to heaven, a look of stern resentment settled on her thin, unsmiling lips. And then there was Hannah, still a baby and placed reluctantly on Mom's lap. With her dark hair and features, she looked nothing like the rest of her fair-skinned, red-headed family, a fact that she had been reminded of often.

"Eat up, Hannah. You'll need your strength." The man at the end of the table ruffled the *Omega Ledger*, his face obscured by the front page.

Hannah glanced down at her plate. A finger. A chunk of flesh. An ear with a gold hoop earring still attached.

She picked up the finger and examined it. "Who is this?"

The man lowered his paper. The dinner table was so long and she was so far away, it was difficult to see his face. But his voice. She knew that voice. It was the one that whispered in her ear. The one that told her that she didn't belong.

"Don't let your mother go to waste, now," he said. "Be a good girl. Eat your pound of flesh."

Hannah gripped her fork and licked her lips. "I can't do it."

The man at the end of the table stood, his form writhing and shifting into a dark mass of smoke. He stretched a great pair of wings as the dinner table and everything on it shook. He roared, the sound reverberating through Hannah's body in a terrifying wave. She clapped her hands to her ears and squeezed her eyes shut.

Wake up. Look who's come to see you.

※ ※ ※

A cawing seagull and the brilliant rays of morning sunlight woke Hannah the following day. She sat upright in a daze as a burning sensation lit her cheek on fire. She slapped at a mosquito, withdrew her hand, and glanced at the thing that had been boring its proboscis into her skin. It was now nothing more than a smear of black and red on her palm. She wiped the insect's remains on the fabric of her jumpsuit and made a face of disgust.

Hannah had attempted to catch a few hours of rest that night on a bench overlooking the water, but her broken sleep had been littered with terrifying dreams. The type of dreams that felt real, like some kind of unlocked memory or premonition. Between the sounds of the night, the din of nearby traffic, and the uncertainty of whether or not she had been followed, Hannah senses had been heightened and her anxiety elevated. She shivered, shook her head, and tried to cast the waning memory of her dream from her thoughts.

Sleeping on a bench down by the river hadn't been the best option, but then again, going back to her hotel room hadn't seemed wise either. The mucky aroma of the Hillsborough River filled her senses, coated her tongue, settled into her lungs, and invaded her thoughts. Claws raked at her insides as a ravenous hunger overwhelmed her. She doubled over, clutched her stomach, and stared into the gray-green water littered with napkins, plastic cups, and straws as a familiar sensation tugged at her chest.

The book was calling to her again.

Hannah stood and surveyed her surroundings; she had somehow ended up at the park after fleeing from Hector's apartment. Vendor trucks had already begun to set up tables and tents along the sidewalk, each of them emblazoned with red, white, and blue for the Fourth of July. Soon the park would be filled with happy families eating hot dogs, soaking up the sun, and waiting for the fireworks display. She hoped to be long gone by then.

Memories of the night before played in her mind on a loop as she trudged through the park toward her hotel, her stomach growling. Teeth. Blood. Wings. Their horrible, ghoulish faces were all still so vivid and real. There would be no going back to work now. No one would believe what she had seen either. Hannah had no other choice but to run again. She *wanted* to be strong. All she wanted was to change her life and do something better. It was time to admit that she was in over her head. Whatever was going on at *Visage Magazine*—whatever *they* were— Hannah didn't care to know anymore. It was time to pack up and go home.

Hannah held her breath as she entered the The Palms, keeping her eyes peeled for any signs of Valerie, Selena, or Fox. She offered the woman at the concierge desk an awkward smile and made a beeline for the elevator. She didn't intend to spend any more time than necessary in the hotel. Her reservation there was all thanks to *Visage* anyway, and they surely knew where to find her. She reasoned that the ghouls wouldn't try anything out in public in broad daylight, and she probably had a little time to kill. All she needed was a quick shower and to pack her few worldly possessions before heading to the bus station and leaving this nightmare behind.

The hot shower was a welcome, warm cocoon. Hannah scrubbed away tiny flecks of gore from her skin as the image of Jeremy's head bursting in Valerie's mouth like a grape played on a loop. She could never tell anyone else what she had seen. No one would believe her. She didn't blame Hector and Alicia for being skeptical. They barely knew her as it was, but then again, no one really knew her. She didn't even know herself.

Hannah exited the shower and was taken aback by her reflection in the hazy mirror. She was still getting used to her new look. She slipped on a comfortable, faded, floral dress and had just finished packing her things when her cell phone rang. She glanced at the caller ID and her blood turned to ice. The number on the screen was one she hadn't seen in a long time, but it was one she knew well. She had recognized that number by heart from the time she was old enough to walk to school on her own.

"Hello?"

"Chastity! We've been so worried about you."

Her throat closed up as she clenched the hot phone in her trembling hand. How long had it been since she had heard her mother's voice? "Mama?"

"Where are you, baby? Everyone's been looking for you."

"I'm coming home, Mama." She swallowed a lump in her throat as fresh tears rimmed her eyes.

"Good, good. But first, you need to eat."

Hannah paused and glanced at herself in the mirror. Her reflection showed her holding her empty hand up to her ear. Her phone lay on the hotel dresser. Something in her shifted.

"This isn't real, is it?"

"Nothing ever is," the voice on the other line said.

"Leave me alone," she said. "You're dead."

The line crackled and the voice deepened. "We're all dead here."

"No!"

"You've always been an abomination," the voice cackled. "You always knew it would come to this."

Stars burst before her eyes in a brilliant flash of light. Hannah fell back on the bed and sunk into the mattress, her senses overwhelmed with the smell of flowers and rot and blood. She drifted into a dark, endless silence, and knew nothing more.

❊ ❊ ❊

The sun was setting outside of Hannah's hotel room window when she woke to the buzzing of her phone. Her eyes flew open and she gasped as the tip of her nose grazed a maze of white, swirling plaster. She held up her hands and pushed against the ceiling, her body crashing back onto the bed.

Hannah sat up and looked around the room, panting. Either she was completely losing her grip on reality or she had just been *floating*.

The phone on her dresser buzzed and lit up again. She stood up, grabbed her phone, and swiped at the screen. She had four missed calls from Hector and a string of missed texts.

Hey, are you OK?

Where are u.

I'm worried about you.

I'm going to the office. I think I figured something out. Meet me there at ten.

Hannah frantically scanned the battery on her phone; it was down to one percent. She sucked in a ragged breath and glanced around her hotel room, unsure of where she had put her phone charger. And then she remembered, her charger was plugged into her computer. At the office. The same place where Hector was heading. *Shit*.

She sat for a moment and stared at the packed duffle bag full of her meager possessions. If she left now, she could be on a bus back home in a matter of hours. She could leave her time at *Visage Magazine* and her fantasy life as Hannah Howarth behind her. Or could she? She could still feel the book pulling at her chest, begging her to go back to the office. Would the book come to find her in Omega? Would her ghoulish co-workers be waiting for her back home?

Hannah glanced at the clock on her bedside table. It was just after nine p.m. An explosion followed by a brilliant burst of light illuminated her darkened hotel room. She rushed to the window in time to see a starburst of sparkles raining down over the Hillsborough River. The Fourth of July fireworks had begun. She had no way to contact Hector without her phone, and had no clue where the nearest big box store was to buy a new one. Against her better judgment, Hannah decided that the last stop before she headed home to Omega was going to have to be Tampa Towers.

She flung her duffle over her shoulder and left the comfort and security of her hotel room toward the last place on Earth that she wanted to be. Her insides groaned as she pressed the elevator button and the doors opened. It occurred to Hannah that she hadn't eaten all day. She rummaged around in her purse for a granola bar and stuffed it in her face as the elevator reached the ground floor. Another loud boom sounded in the distance as she crossed the reception area to The Palms concierge desk.

"Ma'am? Are you checking out?"

Hannah's stomach gurgled as she turned to face the hotel attendant. The man staring back at her was young, probably close to her age. He was fresh-faced and smiling in a way that she found to be both repulsive and hilarious at once. She reached into her purse for the electronic keycard to her room and passed it across the counter as a claw of nausea raked through her guts.

"I... ghlrugh!"

A wave of noxious bile spewed from her lips with tremendous force, spraying the unsuspecting attendant in the face. She braced herself on the concierge counter as the effluence projected uncontrollably from her body like a fire hydrant.

Whatever she was vomiting was the same color, consistency, and aroma as the river water, and the amount that flowed from her body was almost unreal.

Finally, when there was nothing left inside of her, Hannah wiped her mouth with the back of her hand. She felt light again and free, though her head reeled. It wasn't physically possible for that much fluid to be inside of her... was it? The man behind the counter looked every bit as shocked as she was, drenched in whatever it was that had come out of her. Hannah trembled, unsure of what to do or say.

She winced and offered up a weak smile. "Sorry about that."

She turned on shaky legs and bolted toward the door, leaving the attendant bewildered and disgusted. Still hungry, Hannah burst out into the night and ran toward Tampa Towers as a thousand explosions sparkled overhead. In the distance she could hear the cheers of the crowd from the riverside park with every loud boom and explosion. Hannah turned her face up to the night sky and drank in the light of the fireworks, marveling at their magnificent size and sound.

It didn't take long for the pyramid entryway of Tampa Towers to come into view. Just seven days before, she had stood before this very entryway with her face tipped up to the sky. She had been so full of hope that she could pull off this new life as Hannah Howarth, that she could have something good and easy for once. Fate had brought her to

Tampa Towers, and now she feared that everything she had done would be for nothing. She clenched her jaw, zipped past the night guard toward the elevator, and pressed the button for the seventeenth floor. Hannah was starving, and her book was calling.

CHAPTER TEN

The *Visage Magazine* office space was dark and desolate as Hannah made her way through the labyrinth toward her desk. The flash-bangs of the fireworks illuminated her way, throwing shadows on the walls in long, ominous arcs. She passed the photo studio and the glass-front offices of the senior writers, trying not to make a sound. The acrid flavor of river water and bile still coated her tongue, and her thoughts were scattered. She wanted nothing more than to grab her charger, text Hector an apologetic goodbye, and leave Tampa and everyone in it forever.

Claws of hunger raked through her insides as she stumbled down the carpeted hall. It had been a full day since she had kept anything down, yet food was the last thing on her mind. She probably needed to go to the hospital, but she suspected that a doctor couldn't help whatever was going on inside of her. The clench in her stomach doubled her over in pain, causing her breaths to come in sharp and fast. She gagged, her choppy breathing only heightening the dank river water flavor on her tongue.

Hannah entered the office bathroom and flicked on the overhead light. The fluorescent bulbs buzzed and bathed her in a harsh, unflattering glow. She hazarded a glance at her reflection and immediately regretted it. Her chic bob was now matted and stuck out in wild angles around her head. The contents of her stomach stained the front of her dress, and some of it was still crusted at the corners of her lips. Her skin had taken on a grayish pallor and her usually full cheeks appeared gaunt. Another gut-punching cramp tore through her, and Hannah turned on the tap. She splashed her face and rinsed out her mouth, but the flavor of brackish water and acid persisted. Something was happening to her. Something bad.

She stumbled out of the bathroom toward the work station she shared with Hector, but before she had even reached their cubicle, she heard a soft thumping. Hannah froze and something tugged at her heart. She knew exactly what was making all that noise. She stepped into the darkened cubicle as a finale of fireworks exploded in the distance. Hannah turned on the lamp next to her computer and spied her phone charging cord just where she had left it. She slung her bag on the desk, dug her phone out, and plugged it in. Then, something rattled and smacked against the metallic filing cabinet again. She pursed her lips, held her breath, and unlocked the cabinet drawer.

Something small and black escaped from the cabinet on velvety wings, flapping and erratic like a trapped bat finally set free. Hannah let out a gurgly yelp and held up her hands to protect her face as it flew around her head, snapping and screeching. Finally, the creature rested on her desk and went silent and still in the shape of the handbook.

"Told you she didn't read it."

Hannah whipped around at the sound of a chillingly familiar voice. Valerie, Selena, and Fox blocked her exit, each of them shrouded in a red satin cloak. Gone were their wings and unhinged jaws full of shark teeth; the Corporate Coven was back to their aesthetically pleasing, perfect selves.

She grabbed a pen from her desk—the only thing that even remotely looked like a weapon—and held it out in front of her. "Stay back."

"You look like shit, Hannah," Valerie sighed, shook her head, and crossed her arms at her chest. "All of Jean's hard work, gone to waste."

"You should really eat something," Selena chimed in.

"She won't do it," Valerie scoffed. "Look at her. She's too weak."

"Leave her alone, guys," Fox sighed, "Is this really necessary?"

"Are diamond-studded, high-top sneakers necessary? No, but they're fucking cool," Selena snorted. "'*Necessary*'."

"Selena, grab her." Valerie smiled and ran her tongue over a set of perfect teeth.

"Seriously? I spent all morning cleaning up your mess from last night." Selena propped her hands on her hips. "I'm so tired of doing all the heavy lifting."

"Well, you're the one who doesn't want to get a familiar," Valerie replied. "We could get so much more done if we farmed out the work."

"Owning a familiar *is* too much work." Selena shot back.

"Oh, right. And cleaning blood and bits of meat and skin out of Grace's apartment isn't too much work?" Valerie snorted. "But nooo, you just want to be right. Nobody cares!"

"You're not *in charge* you know," Selena sneered. "I've been with Grace just as long as you."

Hannah's eyes flashed to her cell phone as the Corporate Coven squabbled. It was just barely charged—enough for one emergency phone call. She snatched the phone with her free hand and swiped it on. "I'm calling the cops!"

She held her breath, working on instinct alone. She had no plan, no history of bravery to even know if she could carry out her threats. Still, she was cornered and had no other option than to try anything and everything she could. Valerie and Selena ceased their squabbling, turning to look at Hannah. They burst into laughter.

"Oh my God!" Selena cackled. "Do you see her face? '*I'm calling the cops.*' Classic!"

"*Hannah*. Don't be so dramatic." Valerie rolled her eyes. She tossed a red satin gown in her direction. "Here. Make yourself presentable and meet us in Grace's office."

"She's even worse than Jennifer," Selena snorted and turned on her heels.

Valerie and Selena linked arms and turned, laughing in unison and reunited again in their mutual dislike for Hannah. Fox hung back for a moment with a strange expression. For a moment, Hannah felt a sliver of solidarity from Fox.

"Come on, newbie." Fox offered a weak smile. "Don't forget to bring the book."

No sooner had her ghoulish co-workers appeared, they were gone, leaving Hannah dazed and disoriented. She held her phone in one hand and the pen in the other, her gaze resting on the red satin shroud in a pile on the floor. The book had gone still and silent, inconspicuous and innocent as a dictionary. Nothing made sense, and the hunger deep inside of her was only intensifying.

Hannah knew that a call to the cops was important, but reaching Hector was even more urgent. She didn't know what had possessed him to want to come to the office, but she couldn't let him, especially not now. She dialed his number with a shaky hand and glanced at the weird satin shroud, made out of the same cheap polyester used for graduation robes and drugstore Halloween costumes. She bounced on her heels as the phone rang and rang until she finally reached his voicemail.

"Hey, it's Hannah," she whispered. "Don't come to the office! It's not safe here. I need you to call the poli...."

Click.

The call was disconnected. Her cell phone

screen went black in her hand.

"Fuck." Hannah glanced at the handbook again. She knew that she was in way over her head. If she tried to run, they would likely find her anyway. She didn't have a clue what she was doing or what was going on, but she had to do *something*. Against her better judgment, she opened the cover of the handbook and began to read.

At first, the text was just a jumble of characters underneath the ouroboros pentagram, strange markings she had never seen before outside of the book. However, the longer she stared at the page, the more the words began to make sense. The book whispered to her in its ancient language, hissing and lulling her into submission all at once.

The eaters of flesh.
The chosen and divine.
Consume all in their path.
The wicked will....

Hannah slammed the book shut and winced. A stabbing sensation ripped through her right shoulder blade, and she cried out in agony. She reached around, touched her shoulder blades with her fingertips and gasped. Something hard and bony protruded from her back.

"No, no, no, no."

Hannah bolted from her desk toward the bathroom. She gulped in ragged breaths as she burst through the bathroom door and stood in front of the mirror again. She stared at her ragged reflection under the harsh fluorescent lights and pulled her dress over her head. Hannah squeezed her eyes shut and turned around so that her back faced the mirror. In her heart, she already knew what she would see, but she didn't want to admit it.

Hannah opened her eyes as she craned her neck. A choked sob left her body. There, protruding from each of her shoulder blades, was a sharp, hooked claw and the beginnings of a set of leathery, black wings. Defeated, she slipped her dress on and walked back toward her cubicle. She closed her eyes and snorted to herself in a half laugh, half sob. This was what she had wanted, right? She had wanted to change, to become a different person. Well, she got it all right. She was becoming just like *them*.

Hannah wiped at her wet eyes and picked the satin shroud up off the floor. Maybe Jennifer was a smarter intern than she had been. Maybe Jennifer had gotten away. Or maybe they ate her just like they had eaten all of the good-looking people from the nightclub. Either way, Hannah was in far too deep now. She slipped the red cloak over her head, picked up the book, and smoothed down her hair as best as she could.

As she headed toward Grace's office, Hannah realized she might be taking her last steps. She didn't want the beauty, prestige, and power of working at *Visage Magazine* so badly that she would resort to becoming a monster. She *couldn't* join them. She had to figure out some way to destroy them—or be destroyed herself.

CHAPTER ELEVEN

Despite the summer heat, a roaring fire raged in the hearth on the far side of Grace's office. Hannah's eye trailed with suspicion to the mantel, as the flames flickered and cast terrifying shadows all around the editor in chief's dark, somber office. Grace sat at her desk, cloaked in a black satin robe and wearing a dubious grin. Valerie, Selena, and Fox all stood behind her, the hoods of their cloaks partially obscuring their faces.

"Oh, Hannah. What have you done to yourself?" Grace tsk-tsked and rose to greet her with open arms.

Hannah held the book to her chest and flinched as Grace neared. She allowed Grace to fold her into an embrace. For the first time she was able to see her employer up close and was surprised to find her skin was nearly translucent and dappled with blue veins. Her breath smelled of rotting meat as she nuzzled into Hannah's hair.

"Don't you worry about a thing. You just need a good meal and you'll be right as rain."

"No." Hannah pushed her away. "I won't do it."

Grace gave her a sympathetic frown. "I know. It must be hard. Fox was tender-hearted at first like you too."

"I was not," Fox protested.

"Yes, you were," Selena said. "You didn't want to eat that little pink-haired idiot who worked in the mail room." Selena elbowed Fox and mocked in a singsong voice, "she was your *girlfriend*."

"We were just having a good time," Fox demurred.

"Sometimes it isn't as fun to play with our food, that's true." Grace nodded. "But there comes a point where we all have to decide whether to eat or be eaten."

"I don't get it." Hannah glanced down at the book. "What do you want me for?"

"Your youth," Grace said. "I understand this business can seem unpleasant, but someone old-fashioned like myself always benefits from a *fresh* perspective."

"You don't need me for that," Hannah snorted, "you have the Internet."

"Ah yes, but sadly, the people on the Internet don't fulfill our carnal needs and desires. We need to see our subjects in the flesh."

"So, the magazine is just a front for whatever the fuck this is?"

"A honeypot, a spider web, a pyramid scheme. We have many methods of attracting our prey," Grace shrugged. "This one just tends to attract the most delicious types of people."

"It's fucked up is what it is."

"The people we deal with are all bad, Hannah. Vanity. Greed. Desire. Don't think for a moment that you are doing the world a disservice by consuming them."

"You're wrong." Hannah clenched her fists. Jeremy didn't deserve their wrath. She didn't deserve it. "Not everyone is all bad."

Grace chuckled. "There are a few innocents that get entangled along the way, but that's just the price of business. There's *always* collateral damage."

"You can't do this forever," Hannah said. "Someone is going to expose you."

"Well, they haven't yet," Grace said. "We conduct our business in the shadows. Our work is nasty and we need allies that are hungry, but who won't have anyone coming to look for them. People that are easy to mold into our image. People who won't ask too many questions."

"People like me?" Hannah snorted. "That's not who I am."

"Ah, Jennifer thought so too," Grace sighed. "It takes a great deal of vanity, greed, and selfishness to make it in this business. Some of us are meant to die. Some of us are meant to fly."

"So what now?" Hannah threw her shoulders back. If she was going to die, she wasn't going to do it like a coward. "You're obviously not going to let me go. And I won't have any part in this."

"The blood lust isn't that easy to dismiss,"

Grace said, turning her back on her. "Go or stay. It makes no difference to me."

The wall behind Grace's desk opened up to reveal a hidden passageway. Valerie, Selena, and Fox disappeared into the wall and Grace followed them, leaving Hannah alone. She glanced down at the handbook and then at the new opening in the wall. Her hell or her salvation all depended on what she did next. What if the answers existed between the pages of the book? If she left, would she still turn into a ghoul like them? She didn't know the answer.

Just as she was about to toss the book into the flames and run, a voice called out to her from the hole in the wall.

"Hannah!"

Her blood ran cold as she craned her neck and listened. Hector's voice echoed through Grace's office. Any remaining hope she may have had turned to despair.

"Hannah, run!"

She took a deep breath, clutched the book to her chest, and slipped off the satin robe. She couldn't run away. She might not be able to save Hector, but she wasn't going to let him die alone.

❖ ❖ ❖

The long passage behind Grace's office was cool and dark, and the walls were made of raw, unfinished stone. It reminded Hannah of a dungeon. The space opened up to reveal a large chamber illuminated with candlelight. The scene looked like something out of a medieval movie set, with wrought iron accents, velvet curtains, and dozens of candles. An ouroboros pentagram was carved into the floor and Valerie, Selena, and Fox each stood at the end of one of the points of the star. At the center of it all was a man, gagged, and bound to a rolling desk chair. Hector.

"Let him go!" Hannah rushed toward the pentagram circle. Just as she reached the edge of the star, she smacked face-first into an invisible wall.

Selena cackled, "Nice try."

"You can only enter the circle at your designated point, Hannah." Grace was stationed at the top point on the star.

Hector wriggled and moaned, his words muffled under a sagging fabric gag. Selena roughly pushed the gag back into his mouth. "Quit being difficult!"

"Selena, just go get some shipping tape," Valerie whined. "I told you. That fabric gag *never* works."

"*You* go get the shipping tape!"

"Ghouls!" Grace snapped. "You're forgetting yourselves."

Hannah fumed and tried to comprehend the scene that laid out before her. The thought of Hector being ripped limb-from-limb and devoured by these ghouls reignited her rage. Selena and Valerie looked at her, their faces set into a glaring rictus. Fox scowled and stood rigid with clenched fists, their eyes darting from Hannah to Hector. It dawned on Hannah then that this wasn't just any secret chamber—it was a *sacrificial* secret chamber.

Grace's features remained stoic as she summoned Hannah to join them. "Come now, Hannah. You can't fight us."

Hannah glanced down at the book as it pulsed against the palm of her hand. She didn't know the first thing about the occult, spells, witchcraft, or whatever these hags were into. She was just a sheltered runaway from a rural southern town. She had never even seen a Ouija board, watched an R-rated movie, or listened to non-secular music until college. Still, she had to try something, and the book was the only weapon she had. She couldn't let Hector down.

"Hannah!" Grace commanded. "Take your place!"

She opened the book and the pages began the flutter and flip on their own. A great gush of wind howled through the chamber causing the candles to flicker. A low growl came from somewhere overhead, and the pages on the book stopped fluttering. Hannah glanced down at the book and began to read the text of symbols she could barely decipher.

"*Ze Dingir!*"

The floor beneath her shifted and another great gust of wind tore through the circle. The sensation of hot breath scented with sulfur tickled the back of Hannah's neck. Still, the book beckoned her to read.

"*Ze Azag!*"

Another loud roar thundered through the space, knocking the ghouls off their feet and snuffing out the candles. Hannah huffed in disbelief as her co-workers lay writhing on the floor. She had no clue what the words meant or what she did, but whatever it was, it seemed to impair them for a brief moment. She held out a tentative hand toward the circle again and found she was able to cross the threshold.

Hector stared at her with wide, terror-stricken eyes as she struggled to remove his gag. "Hannah! Behind you!"

Fox stumbled toward them, their face contorted in pain. Before Hannah could react, Fox unsheathed a dagger from a belt around their waist and lunged toward Hector.

"No!"

The tip of Fox's blade zipped through the rope around Hector's chest, setting him free. Fox extended the handle of the blade in Hannah's direction. "Here. You're gonna need this."

Another loud roar blasted through the chamber, knocking Fox to the ground. Hector shrugged off his binds, pulled the gag from his mouth, and stood up.

"What's going on?" Hannah glanced toward the exit. Dark plumes of sulfurous smoke began to billow in.

"You just pissed off Azag," Fox said. "We're *so*

fucked."

"How do we get out of here?" Hannah glanced at the exit again. A pair of glowing green eyes pierced through the accumulating wall of smoke.

Fox pointed to the ceiling. A great pyramid of black glass hung overhead. "You can fly."

"How?"

"Hannah." Hector pointed to her shoulder. "You have *wings*."

She blinked, tilted her head to the side and gasped. A dark, leathery object flapped behind her.

This isn't happening. This *couldn't* be happening.

"No, no, no, no, no..." she murmured and opened the book again.

Selena and Valerie rose to their feet, moaning. Grace had vanished.

"Fox, you fucking turncoat!" Selena screamed.

Hannah flipped through the book. "How do I stop this?"

"Read something from the book!" Fox unsheathed a second blade from their belt, hissed and pointed it at Selena.

"Which passage?" Like before, the pages fluttered wildly and stopped at a specific spot. By all accounts, it seemed like the book was actually telling her what to do. She glanced at Fox and then back at the strange text again.

"Read it!" Fox shouted, pointing to the exit of the chamber. "Hurry!"

Hannah held out the book and stared into the

creature's glowing eyes. "*Ze inu!*"

A strangled growl tore through the building. A tremor thundered under their feet, rattling the candles along the wall. The billowing smoke began to recede and another gust of wind ripped through the room. The candle flames flickered back to life and the chamber was quiet once more.

Hannah faced Selena and Valerie with the dagger and the book still at hand. They stared at her gape-mouthed and eyes open wide in twin shocked expressions. Fox hissed at them as they gathered their cloaks and ran out the door.

"Typical," Fox scoffed at their backs.

"Hannah, let's get the hell out of here," Hector whispered.

"*No.*" Hannah flexed her new wings and ran her tongue along a new set of fangs. "Not until I make them pay."

CHAPTER TWELVE

Hannah tiptoed out of the sacrificial chamber with Fox's dagger in one hand and the book in the other, using it as a shield. Hector stayed close to her side, but she made sure to keep Fox at a safe distance. It was less than twenty-four hours ago that she had seen Fox turn some poor woman into a late-night buffet after all. She didn't trust Fox any more than the other ghouls she worked with, and she wasn't about to let Hector or herself become their next meal.

The common area and rows of glass-front cubicles were quiet and still as they wandered through Grace's office and out into the hallway. The digital clock on the wall over the break room showed that it was already nearly morning. Somehow, hours had passed instead of minutes. They had been in the sacrificial chamber for much longer than she'd thought.

"Where do you think they went?" Hannah whispered.

"They're probably hiding." Fox moved to her

side. "You stopped the ritual. The sun is coming up soon, so we won't be as powerful."

"Hey, keep back!" Hannah spat. "Why should I believe anything you have to say?"

"Do you have any better options?"

"No," she admitted. "But you're one of them. This could be some kind of trick."

"Hey, I'm trying to help," Fox said. "I was forced into joining this fucked up coven just like you."

"I don't intend to join anything." Hannah scanned the rows of offices and listened with new sharpened senses. Where would demons go to hide?

Hector shivered and hugged himself. "Why are they hiding?"

"When the sun comes up, we turn to dust," Fox said.

"Wait, so you're like vampires?"

"You know, everything isn't like you see in the movies," Fox huffed. *"Anyways.* No. Not like vampires *at all*. We're former humans possessed by demons that have escaped from the underworld."

"But you *do* eat people," Hector pointed out.

"Unfortunately. Our demons drive us to feed on human flesh so they can survive in our skin. We need souls so we can walk in the daylight, so every year on the Fourth of July, we have to pick the most pure soul we can find and suck it up."

"The Fourth of July?" Hector scoffed. "Shouldn't your soul-sucking sacrificial ritual be on Halloween or New Year's Eve or something like that?"

"I don't know why it's on the Fourth of July!" Fox whined. "I don't make the rules."

Hannah exchanged another confused glance with Hector. "So, is Grace a ghoul too?"

"Yeah. Like the queen bitch of ghouls," Fox continued, "She's some kind of medium between the lords of the underworld. She's been trying to get promoted to official god status forever. I think that's where you come in."

"What was she going to do with me?" Hannah tightened her grip around the dagger.

"Wear your skin, I guess." Fox shrugged. "She tried on Jennifer, but it wasn't a good fit."

"Ew," Hector said. "Poor Jennifer."

"This is so twisted. Ow!" Hannah pivoted and her wings crashed into the wall. She wasn't used to them yet. Not that she ever wanted to be.

"Wait, so I'm the pure soul?" Hector scoffed. "I'm not that pure."

"Yes you are." Fox rolled their eyes dramatically. "You're like a cute little puppy. You would have been delicious."

"So, why did you help us then?" Hannah poked at one of her fangs with her index finger and a wave of nausea hit her. She was still starving and Hector was looking tastier by the minute. If she was turning into one of them, then she'd be dust soon too.

"Because, I'm tired of all this," Fox said. "I never wanted to hurt anyone. The blood lust though… once it's in you, it's hard to control."

"What about that Azog guy?" Hannah said. "Think he'll be back?"

"Only if you summon him." Fox motioned to the book. "Actually, Azog may have forced them out of whatever rock they're hiding under."

"Why would he do that?"

"Grace always warned us to never read the passages about Azog. He's a high-level demon that gets off with dragging other demons back to the underworld."

"What *is* this book anyway?" Hannah opened the cover and flipped through the pages. The handbook was easier to handle now. The soft cover tickled her fingers and almost seemed to purr in her hand like a tame kitten.

"Basically it's a Sumerian early reader," Fox said. "Remember those old-timey Dick and Jane books kids had to read in school?"

"Huh?"

"You know, "See Spot Run" and all that shit?" Fox snorted. "Well that's what this book is, only it's a dead language that can summon demons."

"So it's a demonology book for beginners?" Hector pulled a confused frown.

"Sort of," Fox said. "Only the book reacts to different people in different ways. Grace had us all study the book, but none of us actually figured out how to use it."

"Is there any way to reverse this?" Hannah's throat began to close and tears stung her eyes. The situation was unreal, terrifying, and dire. She didn't want to become a *demon*. She didn't want to wait until morning and turn to dust either.

"Well, as long as you don't eat anyone, you should be good," Fox said. "I've never seen it, but from what I remember in the book, once the sun comes up, if you don't complete the ritual, your demon goes back to the underworld."

"What about you?" she asked. "Is there anything in the book that can cast out your demon?"

"It's too late for me," Fox said. "I gave in to peer pressure and ate people. I'm kind of damned."

"I'm starving," Hannah whimpered. "It feels like my guts are trying to devour me from the inside out."

"If you don't want to turn all the way, you have to resist it," Fox said. "Once you go ghoul, there's no turning back."

"Okay, well, we're doing an awful lot of explaining here and not a lot of doing," Hector said. "I spent my night tied up in a sacrificial chamber. I'd really like to call my girlfriend and go home."

"Oh no!" Hannah cringed. "Do you think she would come here looking for you?"

Hector shook his head. "Probably not. We had a fight because I told her I needed to come to the office and help you. She broke out in hives and took a couple of allergy pills. She's probably knocked out cold."

"Well, we can't risk her coming here." Hannah closed the book. "Let's get you somewhere safe. It's time to hunt these fuckers down."

* * *

Hannah and Fox escorted Hector to the exit of Tampa Towers in silence, her stomach still gurgling and growling as though a wild animal had taken up residence in her gut. She hated to admit it, but the thought of taking a chunk out of Hector's arm or leg crossed her mind for a brief second. Just a nibble couldn't hurt, right? She shivered and forced the thought out of her mind. Getting Hector to safety and far away from her and the rest of the *Visage* staff was for the best. Even if she couldn't save herself, she had to at least try and save Hector.

All the way through the *Visage* offices and out into the lobby, there was no sign of Valerie, Selena, or Grace. Everything was still and suspiciously quiet. Too quiet.

"Are you sure you'll be okay?" Hector turned and glanced at Fox then back at Hannah again.

"Probably not," Hannah said. "You need to get out of here, though. You're not safe here."

"There's a diner a block away. I'll call Alicia from there."

"Tell her I'm sorry," Hannah saidd. "You can call the police if you think you should, but I doubt they'll be much help."

"We'll see." Hector's worried gaze fell on her wings. "You just go deal with those hags."

Hannah gazed up past the palm trees and

through the towering office buildings. The sky was already turning navy. She was running out of time.

"Right. Fox, let's go."

Fox followed her to the elevator. They shared the ride in silence, save for the Muzak playing an eighties pop song overhead. Finally, when they reached the seventeenth floor, Fox cleared their throat and turned to Hannah.

"Before we do this, I just want to let you know that I'm sorry," Fox said. "I wasn't a bad person before all this. And I really did care about Brittany."

"The girl with the pink hair?"

"Yeah," Fox sniffed.

"How long have they been getting away with all of this?" Hannah clenched her fists and winced. Thick claws with pointed, jagged ends had sprouted from her fingertips.

"For ages, I guess. Grace has been shedding skins and running big businesses since the dawn of man."

"Really though? A fashion magazine?" Hannah picked at her claws. "It's a strange venture for demons."

"Not really. Grace was a demon of vanity," Fox said. "Makes sense to me."

"We'll get them," Hannah promised. "For Brittany and for Jeremy, and for everyone else that they've hurt."

Hannah and Fox walked down the hall, past Anton's empty reception desk, past the photo studio and the break room until they were standing in front of Grace's imposing office doors. The shy, timid Hannah that had walked through those doors only a week ago was gone and in her place was a hardened half demon.

She turned to Fox with a stoic smile. "So before I storm in there, I need to know. Is everyone on staff here a demon?"

"No. Just me, Selena, Valerie, and Grace."

"Anton isn't a demon?"

"No. He's just really good-looking." Fox shrugged. "Why?"

"I just want to make sure there's no loose ends. If I'm going to sacrifice myself, I want to make sure I drag every last one of these fuckers back to the underworld with me."

"Even if you do, Grace will be back. The book always finds a way into the hands of someone who is happy to do evil."

"That's actually really depressing," Hannah sighed. "Well, I'm going in. You should stay out here. If I figure out how to summon Azog again, I don't want him sucking your soul back to the underworld."

Fox frowned. "Nah. I'm coming with you. I deserve to be in the underworld."

"Maybe it's not so bad there?" Hannah ventured. "Like, who knows, maybe there are interesting people there?"

"I dunno." Fox shrugged. "This life is hell. Almost anything would be better."

"Sorry you got caught up in all this," Hannah

said.

"Me too."

The light outside was slowly changing color, the navy sky brightening into shades of lavender, pink, and orange at the horizon. Soon, sunlight would stream through the windows and she and Fox would be toast.

"Looks like we're running out of time." Hannah sucked in a deep breath, flexed her wings, and gripped the handle of her dagger. "Let's do this."

CHAPTER THIRTEEN

"Hannah, I'm so disappointed." Grace sat behind her desk filing a set of long, black talons. Her signature long gray hair was gone, and the skin she had been wearing lay in a rumpled heap on the desk before her. The ghoul that lived inside of the editor in chief of *Visage Magazine* was covered in shining scales and boasted an impressive set of needle-like teeth. A velvety set of gray wings were folded elegantly at her sides. Even though the creature sitting before her looked nothing like the infamous Grace Hightower, it still had her voice, her mannerisms, and her body language. The overall effect was chilling, though Hannah was getting used to seeing her co-workers for what they really were. Valerie and Selena stood guard on either side of their mistress like trained dogs. Grace flicked a red-eyed gaze toward Hannah and Fox as they entered her office for what would likely be the very last time.

Hannah stood tall and faced them with her last ounce of bravery. "Sorry, Grace. You were right. I don't think I'm a good fit here after all."

"We gotta stop taking in these spineless interns," Valerie scoffed.

"Fox, I'm not all that surprised by your actions though," Grace said. "You never fully committed to the team."

"I'm putting in my notice," Fox said. "I quit."

"Such a pity," Grace tsk-tsked and turned her attention to Hannah. "Not to worry, you should be easy enough to replace. For now, I have a delicious new flesh suit to try on. The ideal blend of innocence and blasphemy."

Hannah blinked. "You can't mean me."

"Who else would I mean?" Grace's eyes flashed. "You're the perfect abomination."

Hannah's synapses lit up as her mother's dying words echoed in her ears. The sentiment had stung back then. *Abomination.* Over time she had been able to write the accusation off as the crazed delusions of a sick woman high on morphine. Still, whispers followed her after her mother's death and had left a social mark that drove Hannah to keep to herself and cleaved a wedge between her and her family. The feeling of being a cursed outsider had pushed Hannah away from her home and everything she'd ever known. To hear Grace repeat those words felt eerily chilling and prophetic.

"I've been searching for someone like you for a long time. Ingrid really came through for me," Grace said.

Ingrid. Professor Appleton. Hannah's blood

boiled at the notion of being sold out by her college professor. Was there anyone she could really trust?

"So there are more of you out there?"

"We're *everywhere*," Grace hissed. "The face behind every big oil company, every big-box store. You don't get that kind of power without selling your soul."

Hannah exchanged a quick glance with Fox. How many others had Grace run through to get to her? How many other innocent people had she coerced?

"You know, it's not too late. You would make an excellent senior writer for footwear and accessories, Hannah." Grace folded her claws daintily on the desk in front of her. "I can always give Fox's flesh suit a try instead."

"Why?" Hannah squared her shoulders. "What's so great about looking like a human?"

"This is how we survive," Grace sighed and motioned to the pile of skin that had been her body. "That flesh suit is all worn out and too photosensitive. Last season, as they say. Besides, I have to show my face at fashion week in Barcelona next week and Spain is *very* sunny."

"Well, you can't have my body," Hannah said. "I won't let you."

"I'll just have to take it then." Grace waved her hands in a dismissive manner. "Ghouls. Do your thing."

"My pleasure." Selena threw her head back and screeched. Her jaw snapped open like a well-oiled door displaying rows of sharp teeth that protruded from her widening mouth. A pair of leathery black wings burst through her red satin cloak.

Valerie shifted into the same ghoul Hannah had seen the night before, her human features contorting into a gruesome bear trap. The sounds of twisting of bones and stretching skin filled the air as the pair of ghouls lunged toward her and Fox. Hannah jumped out of the way as Selena and Valerie flew through the air with teeth bared and claws extended. Selena tackled Fox to the black marble floor, and the two struggled in a flurry of snarls and flapping wings. The dagger slipped from Hannah's clawed hand. She scrambled toward the blade, but Valerie was too fast.

"Gotcha!" Valerie picked up the dagger and tossed it into the still burning fire. "Now what are you gonna do, rookie?"

Hannah scrambled to her feet, her heart pounding. Suddenly, the pages of the book flew open until they came to rest on a page Hannah hadn't seen yet. She had no other choice than to trust her instinct and read the book.

"*Ash izi!*"

A grinning fireball burst from the hearth, knocking Valerie to the floor. In an instant, her highly flammable, polyester cloak was consumed in flames. Valerie snarled and screeched as she was overtaken by the fire, her not-so-delicate features twisting and melting like wax. Hannah stood with her fists clenched as the ghoul writhed in flames on the floor, morphing into her true, terrifying form as she bubbled and burned. In seconds, the formerly stylish, perky Valerie Beauregard disintegrated into ash.

Hannah pouted at her remains. "Oh no, Val."

"A little help over here!" Fox grunted under Selena's weight.

Hannah glanced at Grace's desk. The glittering ghoul of Grace Hightower had vanished. She turned her attention back to Fox, their face pinched in agony as Selena sunk her claws deeper. She didn't wait to consult the book this time. This time, Hannah worked on pure instinct.

"Hey, Selena," she called.

The Selena ghoul turned her ghastly face toward Hannah and hissed.

"*Ash sag.*"

Selena's glowing green eyes grew wide and bulged in their sockets. A small hiss escaped through her rows of teeth as her head seemed to inflate a little, not unlike a balloon. Her mouth stretched wider and wider until a wet, popping sound filled the air. Selena's head expanded to its very limit until the top of her scalp parted and ripped away. Her skull cracked and red and yellow blood and brains splattered across the room as her head completely exploded.

Fox pushed Selena's headless corpse off and scrambled upright. "How did you do that?"

"I don't know." Hannah glanced at the book, shaking. "It just came to me."

"Where's Grace?" Fox wiped a bit of Selena's blood from their face. "Did you see which way she went?"

Hannah shook her head and gazed toward the door to the sacrificial chamber. "No, but I have an idea."

Fox whimpered. It was then that Hannah noticed a huge chunk of flesh had been ripped from their shoulder. One of their wings was torn and dragging along the floor.

"Selena really hurt you, didn't she?"

Fox nodded.

A guttural, clicking growl bubbled up from deep inside Hannah's throat. "Stay here. I'm going to go take care of Grace."

"How?"

"I don't know," Hannah said. "I'm just moving on pure instinct at this point."

"She'll kill you," Fox said. "She'll try to take your skin and tear you limb from limb, just like she did to Jennifer and who knows how many others."

Hannah shrugged and glanced out of Grace's open office door. Fox followed her line of vision and let out a defeated groan. Bright light spilled into the office through the windows. Morning had come.

"We're toast either way," Hannah said. "Might as well die trying."

"I'm sorry I couldn't help you more," Fox said. "I almost started to believe all of their bullshit."

"I don't think you're a bad person. I got caught up in all of this just like you." Hannah clutched the book to her chest. "Well, I'm going in. Wish me luck."

"Be careful," Fox said. "Don't forget, vanity is Grace's biggest weakness. If you can figure out how to use that, you might have a chance."

"Thanks, Fox," Hannah nodded. "See you on the other side."

Fox coughed. "I wouldn't count on that. It's a nice sentiment though."

Hannah turned toward the darkened entryway of the sacrificial chamber with only the book and her wits for weapons.

CHAPTER FOURTEEN

The sacrificial chamber was pitch black as Hannah entered, the glass ceiling overhead aglow with the first rays of early morning light. Hannah waved her hand as the book whispered in her ear and the candles lit themselves, illuminating the room. There, standing in the center of the ouroboros pentagram was Grace, or rather, the ghoul that she really was. She had shed most of her glittering scales, revealing a thin, dry layer of gray flesh that sagged over angular bones. The few wisps of hair on top of her head stood at attention as though the air was thick with static electricity.

"You're nothing without the gifts I could bestow," she spat, her voice harsh and ragged. "Your skin is wasted on you."

"You're wrong. I'm not nothing."

"Poor, little, country girl in the big city," the ghoul mocked. "I could smell the pig shit on as soon as you walked through the door. You can take the girl off the farm, but you can't ever scrub away the truth."

"I'm not just some dumb farm girl."

"Yes, you are," Grace growled. "That innocent looking flesh suit is the perfect glove for a vile and evil hand. That's why I'm going to take it."

Hannah held the book out in front of her like a protective shield. Her fingernails were long gone, now replaced with shining black claws. Wings had sprouted from her back and she was still so, so hungry. Hannah could never take part in their people-eating activities, but she couldn't live like this either, a ghoul hidden away in the dark. She had nothing left to lose.

"Go ahead," she dared Grace. "I'd like to see you try."

Grace's thin, purple lips drew back into a horrible grin. "My pleasure."

The ghoul flew at Hannah like a bullet with rotten teeth bared and brittle claws raking at her head. The book fell to the floor as Hannah attempted to keep Grace at arms-length. The ghoul's tattered wings beat furiously as she dug into Hannah's scalp.

"Mine!" she hissed, her breath and decaying body foul in Hannah's nose.

She glanced down at the desiccated meat hanging off of Grace's bony arms. Long, needle-like teeth erupted from Hanna's gums and her mouth began to salivate, gushing forth brackish river water. She opened her maw wide and clamped down on Grace's arm, snapping the limb in two.

An ear-piercing shriek escaped from the ghoul's throat and released its grip on Hannah. Black blood oozed slowly from the ragged, open wound as the Grace ghoul recoiled. Hungry as Hannah was, she spit out the cursed meat that filled her mouth. The book lay on the ground, knocked to her feet during the attack. She bent over and picked it up as the ghoul licked at its wound.

"You can't even destroy that which intends to destroy you." The ghoul emitted a low chuckle. "Hannah, however did you expect to make it out here in the great big world?"

"At least I can see myself for what I really am," Hannah spat, her tongue coated in gore. "You couldn't see the truth if it stared you in the face."

"And what truth is that?"

"You're one ugly fucker." Hannah closed her eyes and turned the book to face her. Grace screamed and touched her cheek with her remaining clawed hand, the surface of the book now reflective like a mirror. Grace knocked the book to the ground, heaving and frothing at the mouth.

"You'll never be able to achieve what I have!" she screeched. "You're *nothing*."

"You would have me think that I am nothing," Hannah said. Something warm and bright and powerful was building in her chest. "But it's you. *You're* nothing."

"You're just Chastity Jackson from Omega, Georgia," Grace spat. "Bastard daughter of a pig farmer."

"No," Hannah said, holding the mirror book to her chest. "I did what you suggested, Grace. I studied the handbook. The book told me my true name. I am Ereshkigal. Guardian of the dead and queen of the underworld."

Hannah closed her eyes and she was five again, kneeled down next to her mother as she coughed blood into a handkerchief. Her mother took in a ragged breath, stared at her with vacant eyes and sputtered out two words before collapsing for the final time.

The devil.

In her heart, Hannah had always known who she really was. Her community had always suspected. The book only confirmed it. Now, as she stood before Grace, her human body deformed and the truth out in the open, she could no longer deny the whispers in her ear. She was an abomination. A goddess. A daughter of the devil.

"You *lie*," Grace chuckled, though Hannah detected a hint of doubt.

"Do you know who my real father is?" Hannah opened her eyes and clenched her jaw. "I'll give you a hint. He's got hooves and horns and he's pretty powerful."

"It's not true!" Grace sneered.

Hannah stared down at her, the decrepit ghoul was now a former shell of the powerful editor in chief. Pathetic almost. *Weak.*

"You know, I think working in the industry for so long has made you a little delusional," Hanna mused. "All of this is mine now. It is my right. I'm thinking of taking *Visage* in a new direction."

"You'll never be me." Grace held up an arm to protect herself. "You won't ever live up to my name."

"You're right," she said. "I don't want to."

Hannah waved a hand and just like before, summoned the elements to do her dark bidding. She spread her clawed fingers apart and curled them into a fist, pulling at the invisible strings that held the universe together. She willed the ethereal strands taut between her taloned hands and tied them around Grace's bulbous head, twisting and twisting until her skull burst in an explosion of glitter and black gore.

Blackness surrounded Hannah as the book flew to the ground on its own, landing in the center of the ouroboros pentagram. The pages flipped and a beam of light shot through the air toward the pyramid ceiling. The floor beneath Hannah's feet shuddered as the glass ceiling opened up. She shielded her eyes from the light of the book and glanced up to a galaxy of stars. A shrouded figure stared down at her. A chill ran down her spine as she instinctively knew exactly who she was looking up at.

"Daughter." The dark one leaned over and glanced down at her through the widening hole in time and space. His features were cloaked in darkness and his voice was deep and velvety. *Familiar*. It was the voice behind the whisper that had been with her all of her life.

Hannah frowned. "Hi."

"Are you prepared to take your place?"

She shook her head. "No. I don't want it."

"You wish to stay here?"

"I do."

The dark one let out a deep, guttural laugh. "Such a pity. Earth is the real hell, you know?"

"I know." Hannah glanced through the infinite darkness toward the door and contemplated for a moment. He was right. It was terrifying out there in the big, wide world. Everything was a struggle. People were awful to one another. Still, she thought of all of the things she had yet to experience, the friendships she had yet to make, and places she had yet to see. There were good people out there, people who didn't deserve to be fodder for the likes of Grace and her band of ghouls. There was a whole world out there to explore. She wasn't ready to give all that up yet.

"Join me, daughter." The dark one reached down through the portal, extending a long, bony arm. "You won't get another opportunity."

"I'll stay."

"Hmm." The dark one retreated in a flurry of bones and billowing black robes. "Suit yourself."

Adrenaline flooded her veins. She paused and ventured a request. "I do have one favor to ask."

"How amusing." The near hint of a smile broke through the darkness. "Go ahead."

"Give Fox immunity," she demanded. "I wouldn't have been able to defeat Grace without my friend's help."

The dark one pondered a moment. "The Azag

will be disappointed."

Hannah shrugged.

"Fine. Granted." With that, the dark one waved his hand and dissipated into a plume of dark smoke. The swirling crevasse above her shifted and closed, the eye of the universe tightening until there was only the pyramid ceiling once again. Hannah picked up the book from the pile of glittery ashes and exited the sacrificial chamber for the very last time.

CHAPTER FIFTEEN

Hannah crouched next to the still burning fire in Grace's office with the handbook curled in the palm of her hand. It was warm and pulsed beneath her touch, cozy against her hand and trusting her. Needing her. Though it pained Hannah to let the book go, she knew that it was no good. She couldn't keep it in her possession, and she couldn't let anyone else find it either. It must be destroyed or she knew that it would destroy her.

Fox limped over from the shadows and stood next to the fireplace. "What happened?"

"Grace is gone," she said. "You won't have to worry about her anymore."

"I wouldn't be so sure of that." Fox shuddered. "Still, it does feel different here, doesn't it?"

Hannah breathed in a deep lungful of air and nodded. "Yeah. It does."

Fox glanced at the book. "What are you going to do with that?"

"Throw it in the fire," Hannah sighed.

"Are you sure that's a good idea?"

"It's the only idea I've got." Hannah said a silent goodbye to the cursed book and tossed it into the flames. She half expected it to screech and fly back out at her, refusing to be consumed by the flames. Instead, the book just sat on top of the burning logs, innocent as a school textbook. Hannah almost felt sad as its cover began to singe and curl up at the edges.

Hannah glanced back at Fox. "Come on. Let's get out of here."

"I can't," Fox said. "I have to hide here until dark or I'm toast."

Hannah smiled and nodded in the direction of Fox's shoulder. "What if I told you that you didn't have to?"

Fox glanced at the shoulder that Selena had taken a bite out of and gasped. The ragged, exposed flesh was beginning to hew back together. Fox's wings cracked and crumbled away, falling to the ground as dust. In the blink of an eye, her friend was restored to their human form. Hannah brushed at her own shoulders and flung off her wings as though they were made of sand. She ran her tongue along the flat ridges of her human teeth and smiled.

"Whoa!" Fox glanced down at their claw-free hands. "How did you do that?"

Hannah shrugged. "Someone powerful owed me a favor."

"I don't deserve this though." Fox walked toward the window and parted the heavy purple curtains. Soft morning sunlight streamed in, and

Fox drank in its beautiful warmth.

"Yes, you do," Hannah said. "Good people deserve a second chance."

"Thank you," Fox said. "I'm not going to waste this."

"I know you won't." Hannah's stomach growled. She frowned and for a moment, a slight wave of doubt crossed her mind. She was hungry, but it wasn't *that* kind of hunger. It was just the regular, normal human hunger she was used to. "So, what now?"

"Now I go back to Miami and find my mom and my brother," Fox said, walking toward the door. "I have some lost time to make up for. What about you?"

"I don't know," Hannah said, glancing around the *Visage* offices. The handbook had told her many horrible things about her true nature, including all that the dark one bestowed upon her. The entirety of Tampa Towers was, by birthright, hers to do with as she wished. The portal to the universe, the sacrificial chamber, Grace's old office. She could have it all. Only she didn't want it.

"I'll figure out what I want to do," she said. "For now, let's just get out of here."

Hannah and Fox rode the elevator down to the ground floor for the last time, enjoying a quiet, shared silence. She caught a glimpse of herself in the reflective surface of the elevator, all disheveled dark hair and bangs. Chastity. Hannah. Ereshkigal. She was none of them and all of them. Perhaps she could start over somewhere else as Hannah Howarth. Or stay. Maybe Tampa wasn't such a bad place after all.

"I think I'll go back to my apprenticeship at that tattoo parlor," Fox said. "I could open up my own shop down in Ybor."

"That would be nice," Hannah nodded.

"What are you going to do?"

"I don't know," she said. "Anything. Everything."

The elevator doors opened, and she and Fox linked arms as they strode through the lobby of Tampa Towers. Two police officers barrelled through the front doors, paying them no attention and heading toward the elevator. Fox and Hannah exchanged confused glances as they exited the pyramid vestibule out into the sidewalk.

"What was that all about?" Fox asked.

"Hannah!" Hector waved and shouted to her from across the street. "Hannah! Quick! Get over here!"

Hannah unlinked her arm with Fox's and they crossed the street. She wrapped her arms around Hector's neck and squeezed him in a hug. "You're okay!"

"Yeah, I'm sorry. I made an anonymous call to the cops. I didn't tell them anything, just that someone was in danger on the top floor."

"Does Alicia know you're safe?"

"Yeah. She's a little pissed, but I think she'll be happy that I'm not going back to work there," Hector said. "I was hoping maybe you could help me do some damage control and explain some things to her?"

"Of course! Are you okay, though? Like, really truly okay?" Hannah asked, her brow furrowed with worry. Hector had spent the night tied up and tortured by ghouls. Any person would be an emotional wreck after an ordeal like that.

"I'm a little shook up, but I'm grateful. You saved me," Hector smiled. "Anyway, Alicia is waiting for us at the diner. Will you both come have breakfast with us?"

Hannah smiled and nodded, "I would like that."

She glanced back up at Tampa Towers, no longer intimidated by the building and the things and people within. Hannah had expected her internship at *Visage Magazine* to change her, but not like this. She glanced around downtown with newborn eyes as they walked and she noticed that the colors were more vibrant. The scent of ozone and asphalt and earth hit her nostrils a little differently. Even the atmosphere, sticky and hot, pressed down on her in a pleasant sort of way. Earth was hell. But it was hers. And she was glad to be there.

"There's something I have to tell you," she admitted as the diner came into sight. "My real name isn't Hannah."

"Yeah it is," Fox smiled. "Your name is whatever you want it to be."

Hannah nodded and a warm, honey feeling spread through her chest.

"So, what are you going to do now?" Hector asked.

"Get a different job, I guess. I know I'll never work in an office again though."

Hector snorted, "Yeah, no way. Corporate jobs are a living hell."

Fox held open the door as they reached the diner, and the scent of bacon and biscuits greeted them. A server smiled at them as they walked in, and Alicia waved from a booth, a look of concern painted on her face. Hannah didn't know what the future could possibly hold for someone like her, but she knew one thing: right now she had friends. She had herself. And pretty soon, she was going to get something to eat. Finally.

EPILOGUE

"Hey, what's this?" Officer Jones stooped over in the darkened office on the seventeenth floor and squinted. The flames of a dying fire flickered along the cover of a singed black book in the center of the room.

"I dunno. I think this was a crank call. There's no one here." Officer Eckles took out his walkie. "Let's get outta here."

"What the hell *is* this?" Jones picked up the book and the cover buzzed against his fingertips.

A crackle of static electricity raced up his arm as the pages of the book fluttered open and a deep, reassuring voice whispered in his ear.

About the Author

Wendy Dalrymple is a multi-genre author of Florida gothic horror and contemporary romcoms. When she's not writing happily-ever-afters and tropical thrillers, you can find her camping with her family, painting (bad) wall art, and trying to grow as many pineapples as possible. Keep up with Wendy at www.wendydalrymple.com or follow her on Twitter @wendy_dalrymple.

BOOKS BY THIS AUTHOR

White Ibis

"Truly terrifying" - Jenna Dietzer, author of "The Lovebugs"
"Creepy as hell" - Sheri L. Williams, author of "Forest of Blood'

Obsession. Lies. Greed.
Chelsea is vain, self-absorbed, driven in life only by want and her obsession with being the best. However, despite wanting to portray an outwardly perfect image, things at home are crumbling between her and her boyfriend, Brendan. Together they harbor a secret that has been slowly chipping away at their relationship, and now, things have come to a breaking point.

One day at yoga class, Chelsea meets a woman named Damaris who is exactly like her; beautiful, confident, and reaching high to be her best self.

Damaris and Chelsea become instant best friends and bond over healthy eating, fitness, and their love of luxury items. As Chelsea's heart hardens toward her boyfriend, her obsession with the enigmatic Damaris only blossoms.

As one bad decision turns into another, Chelsea begins to think she is being followed by a white bird. Her new best friend Damaris suggests a girls' weekend in New Orleans to get away from it all and Chelsea readily agrees. Unfortunately for Chelsea, it soon becomes clear that she can't run away from her problems and instead finds herself tumbling head-first into a downward spiral.

They Come From The Water

Family secrets, grief and a dark, foreboding mystery...

Estranged sisters Summer and Joy are forced to reunite after the untimely and gruesome deaths of their mother and grandparents. The two sisters are tasked with cleaning out their grandparents' home on Palmetto Lake in the heart of Central Florida during the hottest, most brutal time of the year. But something seems amiss in the bucolic lakefront community. Something Summer can't seem to place her finger on.

Despite decades of unspoken animosity, the two

sisters attempt to come together to support each other as they uncover the terrors of their unknown past. Questions about the true nature of their grandparents and the strange lakefront neighborhood bubble to the surface as Summer struggles to stay focused on the task at hand.

However, with every layer the sisters strip away, with every new bit of evidence about their grandparents that they stumble upon, it becomes more and more clear to Summer that they aren't just going dealing with grief and loss... but danger. When it comes to the past, sometimes the truth is better left unknown.

They Come From the Water is a Florida Gothic meditation on inherited family trauma, destructive secrets and dark dangers that lurk just beneath the surface.

*Content warnings: Addiction, adultery, murder, suicide, self-harm, animal death and gore.

Roser Park

"Readers who enjoy a spine-tingling gothic with modern flair will relish this haunted house tale. I raced to the end because I simply could not wait to see what happened next! The events at Roser Park will have you leaving the lights on and checking all your doors. Deliciously tense!"

--Paulette Kennedy, author of Parting the Veil

"A fun, modernized Gothic romance with all the elements of a classic
haunted house story and plenty of twists and turns."
--Laurel Hightower, author of Below

Charlotte Slater is freshly divorced and starting over again in her hometown of St. Petersburg, FL. When a dog sitting job in the nearby upscale neighborhood of Roser Park falls in her lap, Charlotte jumps at the chance to make some easy money and enjoy a little peace and quiet. But as usual, when things seem to be too good to be true, they often are.

While the job seems fine on the surface, from the moment Charlotte crosses the threshold at 684 Roser Park Drive, she can't shake the feeling of being watched. The homeowner's nearest neighbor, Adam, always seems to be lurking just around the corner, and soon, Charlotte can't get the handsome, mysterious landscaper out of her thoughts to the point of near obsession.

As each day passes, Charlotte becomes more uneasy in the big, ominous home, causing her to spiral further and further into her own self-doubt. Items aren't where she left them, her senses feel off, thoughts are fuzzy and an imposing painting in the living room calls out to her. A strange force from inside the very walls beckons her to learn the secrets of Roser Park and dig deeper into a century old mystery forgotten by time. Even as danger lurks just outside her door, Charlotte must choose between her instincts and common sense if she wants to ever leave the house alive.

Made in United States
North Haven, CT
13 July 2023